YS OPF

THE SIX CROWNS

FAIR WIND TO
WIDDERSHINS

THE SIX CROWNS

ALLAN JONES GARY CHALK

GREENWILLOW BOOKS
An Imprint of HarperCollins*Publishers*

+
Fiction
Jones

The Six Crowns: Fair Wind to Widdershins
Text and illustrations copyright © 2010 by Allan Frewin Jones and Gary Chalk

First published in 2010 in Great Britain by Hodder Children's Books, an imprint of Hachette Children's Books. First published in 2011 in the United States by Greenwillow Books.

The right of Allan Jones to be identified as the author and Gary Chalk as the illustrator of this work has been asserted by them.

The text of this book is set in Transitional 521 Bitstream
Book design by Sylvie Le Floc'h

Library of Congress Cataloging-in-Publication Data
Jones, Allan Frewin, (date).
Fair wind to widdershins / by Allan Jones ; illustrated by Gary Chalk.
p. cm. — (The six crowns)
"Greenwillow Books."
Summary: Hedgehogs Trundle and Esmeralda, along with their new friend Jack Nimble, sail out into the Sundered Lands to find Esmeralda's aunt, who they hope will help them unravel the clues to find the next of the six crowns.
ISBN 978-0-06-200626-4 (trade bdg.)
[1. Adventure and adventurers—Fiction. 2. Aunts—Fiction. 3. Prophecies—Fiction. 4. Badgers—Fiction. 5. Hedgehogs—Fiction. 6. Animals—Fiction.]
I. Chalk, Gary, ill. II. Title.
PZ7.J67795Fai 2011 [Fic]—dc22 2010049000

11 12 13 14 15 CG/RRDB 10 9 8 7 6 5 4 3 2 1
First Edition

 Greenwillow Books

Six are they, the Badgers' crowns.

If power ye seek, they must be found.

Crystal, iron, and flaming fire—

Gather them, if ye desire.

Ice, and wood and carven stone—

The power they give

Is yours

Alone.

PROLOGUE

The legends say that once—long, long ago—there was a single round world, like a ball floating in space, and that it was ruled over by six wise badgers. The legends also tell of a tremendous explosion, an explosion so huge that it shattered the round world into a thousand fragments, a vast archipelago of islands adrift in the sky. As time passed, the survivors of the explosion thrived and prospered and gave their scattered island homes a name—and that name was the Sundered Lands.

That's what the legends say.

But who believes in legends nowadays?

Well . . . Esmeralda Lightfoot, the Princess in

Darkness, does, for one. According to Esmeralda, the truth of the ancient legend was revealed to her in a reading of the magical and ancient Badger Blocks—a set of prophetic wooden tokens from the old times. And her reluctant companion, Trundle Boldoak, is beginning to believe, as well—especially as they have already found the Crystal Crown, first of the six lost Badgers' Crowns. They also have a new friend to accompany them on their quest—a light-hearted minstrel by the name of Jack Nimble.

But there is a problem. Someone else is also hunting for the six Badgers' Crowns. His name is Captain Grizzletusk, and he's the meanest, bloodthirstiest, wickedest pirate ever to sail the skies of the Sundered Lands. And worse than that—he's hot on their trail. In fact, he's right behind them!

On the Twelfth Day of Greengrow

"Hold on tight!" yelled Esmeralda. "We have to tack! Release the windward jib sheet and keep your head down!"

"What?" screeched Trundle, clinging on for dear life as the little skyboat heeled over and made a tight curve around a chunk of floating rock. "I don't know what that means!"

"I do!" shouted Jack. "Leave it to me!"

He snatched hold of a rope and raced from one

side of the skyboat to the other, dragging the long boom along behind him. The sail snapped and emptied of wind, falling slack against the mast.

The skyboat stalled in the air, throwing Trundle forward so he bumped his nose on the mast. "Ow!" he yelped. "Steady on!"

"Well done, Jack!" yelled Esmeralda. "Now transfer the sail!"

Jack raced back, almost trampling on Trundle on the way.

"Hey! Careful!" Trundle yelped, ducking as the boom came sweeping back over his head.

The wind caught it, and they were off again, darting like an arrow through the rock-strewn sky.

"Nice going, Jack!" howled Esmeralda. "That'll show 'em!"

Trundle peered over the stern of the skyboat. For a few moments, all he could see was the fast-receding chunk of rock, but then a fearful sight hove into view: a great ironclad pirate windship, its bloodred sails billowing and straining, its hull bristling with cannon.

"They're still coming!" howled Jack.

"I'll jibe 'em till their eyes spin!" shouted Esmeralda. "We'll fill the sail on a new tack, then we'll run before the wind!"

"But that will mean going straight into the middle of the Goills!" shouted Jack, sounding alarmed.

"I know!" hollered Esmeralda. "That's the whole point!"

Clutching on to the mast, the wind whistling about his ears, Trundle turned to look ahead. His legs buckled and his prickles stiffened with fear at the sight that met his eyes.

The whole sky ahead of them teemed with massive rocks and boulders, and with great fists and crags of stone that stretched out in all directions.

This was the dreaded Goills—a scattering of sky

rubble into which no sane sailor would ever venture. Trundle had read about the place in books, but he had never imagined being taken into it.

Especially not by a reckless Roamany girl who was more than half out of her mind! They'd be driven onto the rocks by the vicious whip of the wind. They'd be smashed to fragments.

Esmeralda leaned hard on the tiller, and the tall sail filled with wind. Ropes strained. The mast creaked. The boom shuddered.

A lump of rock the size of a house loomed up straight ahead. Trundle huddled down and closed his eyes tight. He felt the skyboat swerve to one side, and when he looked again, the rock was behind them and they were racing through the Goills like a feather on the wind.

"You're crazy!" yelled Trundle.

"I'm brilliant!" shouted Esmeralda, her eyes gleaming.

"She's both!" hollered Jack. He laughed wildly,

pointing back. "Look at 'em! They daren't follow us! We've done it, we've outrun 'em!" And he fell on his back in the keel and waggled his legs in the air.

He was right. The *Iron Pig* had come about, its red sails quivering as they lost the wind. The pirate ship was too big and unwieldy to venture into the Goills.

A figure stood at the bows of the dreadful ship, and a voice came howling across the air to them. "This ain't over, you scurvy snippets! Run while you can! We'll feast on your livers yet!"

Filled with a sudden angry courage, Trundle got to his feet, hanging on to the mast with one hand, shaking his fist and yelling at the top of his voice.

"Come on, you cowards! What's wrong? Scared of a few pebbles, are you?" He took a deep breath. "You can't sail for toffee!" he bellowed into the wind.

"Don't taunt the pirates," warned Esmeralda. "They have long memories, Trundle, and they're not going to give up."

Trundle looked uneasily at her. "But we're safe now, aren't we?"

Esmeralda nodded. "I think so," she said. "Safe from Captain Grizzletusk and his scurvy crew, at least. But we're not out of trouble yet. Jack! Get up and man the boom, there's a good fellow! The Goills isn't known as the windships' graveyard for nothing!"

It was tricky going at times, but with Esmeralda yanking on the tiller and yelling commands, and with Jack hauling at the ropes and Trundle hanging on for all he was worth, they eventually emerged safe and sound on the far side of the Goills.

With danger left far behind and with a fresh wind blowing into its bulging sail, the *Thief in the Night* went skimming jauntily along through a clear, pirate-free sky.

It was at about this point that Trundle ventured a question or two.

"Where exactly are we going?" he asked, looking hopefully at Esmeralda. "Only, I was thinking, I'd quite like to pop back home . . . just for a little while, you know. For a bit of a rest after all we've been through."

"I'm all for rest and relaxation," said Jack, lying in the bottom of the skyboat with his arms behind his head and his feet up on the bow rail. "I know a tavern keeper in Hernswick Town—a sweet soul called Corrie Cutthroat. You'd like her, she's a sport! She'd give us a fair deal on bed and board. Why, there was this one time—"

"Sorry, no can do." Esmeralda interrupted him. "We've got to find Aunt Millie first and show her that iron key we found with the Crystal Crown. My guess is it opens a secret room or a locked chest where the Iron Crown has been hidden for thousands of years. And I'm betting Aunt Millie will know just exactly where it is! With her help, we'll track down the rest of the crowns in no time!"

"Yes, but . . ." Jack and Trundle began together.

"I'm going to take us to Tenterwold," said Esmeralda. "The Roamany caravans will be there—and so will Aunt Millie!"

"How do you know that for sure?" ventured Trundle.

"Because it's almost the twelfth of Greengrow!" said Esmeralda. "The Roamanys always arrive in Tenterwold on the twelfth of Greengrow for the start of the Annual Port Tentercombe Cheese Fair!" She rolled her eyes. "Don't you know *anything*?"

Three days out from the Goills, early on a bright and sunny morning, Esmeralda suddenly let out a yell and pointed over the starboard side of the skyboat.

"We're here!" she whooped. "That's Tenterwold. Can I navigate, or what?"

Trundle and Jack peered over the bow. A lush green island was rising rapidly up beneath them.

From that height, it seemed to be a land entirely made up of gentle hills and valleys and of patchwork fields and cultivated woodlands.

"Sweet!" said Jack, winking at Trundle. "Sweet as a nut!"

Making easy landfall, they moored their skyboat at a quay on the outskirts of a charming little town that lay in a wide valley of meadowlands and pastures. Forested hills rolled along the far horizon, and the sky above was bright with fluffy white clouds.

Trundle gazed happily around himself as they headed into the bustling town of Port Tentercombe. The crown and key were stowed safely away in a sack that hung over his shoulder. How very pleasant, Trundle thought to himself, sniffing at the fragrant air. And such a change from the stinky, crime-infested warren of Rathanger and the dark and dismal mines of Drune!

A festive crowd of friendly folk surrounded them, buzzing with excitement and anticipation. The big event was about to get under way. The whole town was festooned with garlands and bunting in bright greens and yellows, and with banners and posters proudly proclaiming:

The 100th Annual Port Tentercombe Cheese Fair!
Opening Ceremony on Trelawny Green At Noon on the Twelfth of Greengrow

"And the twelfth of Greengrow is *today*," Esmeralda told them. "And it's a tradition among us Roamany folk to roll the first new cheeses of the season. The caravans should arrive anytime now! Aunt Millie would never miss the opening day of the Port Tentercombe Cheese Fair!"

Trundle looked thoughtfully at her. She was convinced that her aunt would help them in their search for the magical crowns of the badger lords of old. What Trundle hoped was that Esmeralda's aunt would prove to be a sensible and level-headed woman who would tell her to stop chasing fairy tales and who would take Trundle back home.

Well . . . *part* of Trundle hoped for that—the cautious part of him that he had spent most of his life listening to. But deep inside him, there was another Trundle, who yearned for far horizons and bold adventures and noble quests.

Sometimes Trundle really wished his inner Trundle would just shut up and go read a book or something! But then Trundle's paw would stray onto the hilt of his newfound sword, and heroic thoughts would bubble up in him and make his head feel a little woozy.

It was all rather confusing really, and Trundle was torn between wanting to thumb a lift on the next windship back to Shiverstones, and a rather worrying desire to follow this mad quest through and find the other five crowns.

As though in response to his thoughts, Jack began
to sing at the top of his voice.

The Badgers of Power, they had six magic crowns
Of crystal, iron, fire, cold ice, wood, and carved
stone.
And brave is the beast who can hunt the crowns
down—
But no beast can do this who travels alone.

O'er stepping-stone islands, by skyboat and sail,
Pure must the hearts be that follow the trail.
For great is the treasure that waits at quest's end—
The sundered worlds bonded, the bad spell to mend.

So quickly, you brave hearts, lest evil gets its hour,
For great is the measure of Badgers' old power.

As the song came to an end, a passerby tossed a
coin.

"Thank you kindly," Jack called, catching the coin with a deft flick of the wrist. "Ah, but it's grand to be able to sing again!" A hint of regret entered his voice. "I'd give these fine folk a merry tune, too, if only my dear old rebec hadn't been smashed by those filthy rotters in the mines!"

Trundle was about to ask what a rebec was when Esmeralda let out a triumphant whoop. "Aha!" she hollered. "Just what we need!"

She was pointing toward the ornate white stone facade of a large shop that loomed ahead of them like an extravagant wedding cake. A sign hung above the pillared entrance.

THE PORT TENTERCOMBE
GENTS' AND LADIES' OUTFITTERS
BESPOKE AND OFF~THE~PEG
CLOTHING AND EQUIPMENT
TO SUIT EVEN THE MOST
SEASONED OF TRAVELERS

"I'm sick of these rags and tatters we've been wearing!" Esmeralda added, marching across the road. "Let's get kitted up!"

Trundle had to admit she had a point— Esmeralda's and Jack's clothes were filthy and torn from their time in the mines of Drune, and even his own jacket and trousers looked much the worse for wear following their recent escapades.

"Follow me!" she called over her shoulder, running up the marble steps and pushing through the double doors. "Service!" She flourished a wad of paper sunders. "Come along—shake a leg! You've got customers here!"

They left the Port Tentercombe Gents' and Ladies' Outfitters some two hours later, decked out in the very finest explorers' clothing. They had also arranged for a whole heap of goods and provisions to be taken off to Pooter's Quay, where the *Thief in the Night* was moored.

Feeling rather smart with his sword hanging from a brand-new shining leather belt, and with the Crystal Crown and the key tucked safely away in a multipocketed backpack, Trundle headed along the high street with Jack on one side and Esmeralda on the other. The hunt was now on for an inn or hostelry where they could get something to eat and drink while they waited for the Roamany caravans to arrive.

They decided against the Stinky Blue Tavern and the Cheese That Walked Alone Hotel and opted instead for the Bountiful Udder Inn. A few minutes later, they were sitting in the beer garden, basking in the sunlight, eating cheese rolls and swigging fresh milk and watching the clouds go waltzing across the sky.

But delightful as all this was, Trundle couldn't help himself from occasionally looking up uneasily into the vast, endless skies of the Sundered Lands. He could see a few of the neighboring islands hanging in the deep blue, some so close he could actually make out shapes and colors, others so far away that they were no more than black dots.

He was scouring the sky for a big ironclad windship with bloodred sails and a crew of savage, murderous pirates. One or two windships were scudding blithely among the clouds, their sails plump with the wind, their flags fluttering. But of the fearsome *Iron Pig*, there was no sign. So far.

"Are you *sure* we lost them?" Trundle asked for probably the fiftieth time in the past few days.

Esmeralda Lightfoot sighed and rolled her eyes.

"Trundle," she said, "you're a good fellow, but you're such a worrywart! I told you—there's no way the *Iron Pig* could have followed us here."

"She's right," added Jack Nimble, giving Trundle an encouraging grin. "We outran them salty bilge rats, sure and certain."

Trundle eyed the traveling minstrel uneasily. Jack was always optimistic. Trundle found it hard to trust someone who constantly looked on the bright side. It wasn't natural.

Esmeralda gave Trundle an encouraging pat on the back. "Have some faith," she said. "Have I ever let you down?"

Trundle gazed at her. "You dragged me from my home and almost got me killed by a mob of rampaging pirates," he reminded her. "Then you hauled me off to the mines of Drune, where I was chased from teatime till breakfast by an angry mob, almost carved into slices by a demented bosun, nearly squished flat by a cave-in, and then all but blown to smithereens by blackpowder."

"All true," Esmeralda admitted. "But it was the prophetic Badger Blocks that set everything in motion. You know that. And we did find the Crystal Crown."

"Yes, we did," Trundle conceded.

"And there *was* a clue with the crown to help us find the next one."

"There was a *key*," said Trundle. "As to whether it's a clue . . ."

"It is," insisted Esmeralda. "Trust me!"

"If you say so."

"And on top of that, we freed the slaves from the mines," Esmeralda added.

"That you did!" said Jack. "And right glad I am of it, I can tell you! All that dust and grime—it was playing havoc with my vocal cords!" He coughed and thumped his chest. "But I can feel them improving by the hour!"

"And did I get us away from Grizzletusk?" Esmeralda continued. "And did I navigate safely through the Goills? And did I bring us here on the very day that Aunt Millie and the Roamany caravans will be arriving?" She beamed at him. "Look around you, Trundle! This is a lovely place. Relax! Enjoy yourself! Everything is fine. Nothing can possibly go wrong!"

Trundle took a long, deep breath. Maybe she was right. Maybe he was fretting over nothing. He returned his gaze to his plate and took a large bite of his cheese sandwich.

"I say!" announced Jack, pointing up into the sky. "What's *that*?"

Trundle almost choked. "What's what?" he coughed, staring up in alarm. *"Pirates?"*

"No," said Jack. "That! Or rather—*them!*"

A murmur of excited voices was rising up all around them as other people looked to see what was approaching.

Trundle peered upward, shading his eyes with one paw. He let out a breath of relief. He couldn't quite make out the new arrival, but it certainly wasn't the *Iron Pig*.

At first it looked like a string of dark pearls, threading its way across the high sky. Then, as it snaked and looped down between the bubbling white clouds, it looked more like a collection of matchboxes tied together.

And finally, as the procession swooped and dived right over the rooftops of Tentercombe, Trundle saw with a thrill of delight and excitement that it was a linked line of colorful Roamany caravans, drawn along by a windship with crimson sails. The caravans shone with reds and greens and blues and yellows, their sides picked out with scrolls of painted woodwork and covered with swirling patterns and designs and big, bold lettering. And instead of wheels, Trundle saw that all the Roamany caravans had long wrought-iron skids.

Roamany men and women and children hung from open doors and windows, shouting and blowing trumpets and throwing down confetti and waving to the crowds that had come out onto the streets to greet them.

Trundle and Jack and Esmeralda ran into the middle of the street and cheered and waved and jumped up and down with glee as the glorious caravans circled overhead.

The string of caravans performed a long loop over the high street, then went sweeping away, descending into a wide meadow before coming to a slow, sliding halt while the people of Port Tentercombe went racing off to greet the exotic newcomers.

"Let's go!" yelled Esmeralda, almost bowling Trundle over as she whizzed past him. "We have to get to Aunt Millie straightaway. She'll help us work out where the next crown is—no problems!"

Trundle and Jack looked at each other for a moment, then chased after her.

After everything he had been told, Trundle was rather looking forward to meeting Esmeralda's famous aunt.

2

Plum Cake
and
Strawberry Tea

"Well! This is something like, I must say!" declared Jack, grinning like a piano. "I haven't been to a Roamany fair in years!"

"Wonderful!" Trundle gasped. "It's absolutely wonderful!"

No sooner had the line of caravans come to a graceful curving halt than their doors were flung wide and their sides burst open and, as if by magic, the meadow was suddenly filled with colorful pavilions and sideshows and fairground booths and tents and attractions. The air rang to the sound of pipe organs and flutes and drums and tambourines and voices calling and laughter and the smells of toffee apples and candyfloss and boiled sweets.

Trundle saw Esmeralda in among the crowd, racing from booth to booth, from sideshow to sideshow, leaping about and shrieking for joy and flinging her arms around the necks of the brightly dressed Roamany folk, as though intent on hugging every single one of them. It was clear from their reactions that they were overjoyed to see her, too. And no wonder: the last time they had laid eyes on her was when she was being dragged away by marauding pirates. Trundle guessed that most people kidnapped by pirates never came home again, ever.

But then most people weren't quite as resourceful as Esmeralda Lightfoot.

Jack linked his arm with Trundle's, and the two of them stepped out into the riotous fairground. As they strolled among the attractions, cheery voices rose up all around them.

"Try your luck, my bonny young fellows!"

"Three throws for a sunder!"

"Roll up, roll up! You have a lucky look about you, my lads! Throw a hoop and win a prize!"

"Popcorn! Buttered or salted or smothered in honey!"

"Your fortune told—only two sunders!"

"Genuine sharks' teeth from the dark lagoons of Gnashenchopper's Reef! They'll bring you good luck!"

Trundle gaped at the alluring signs that adorned the sides of many caravans.

Hattie Hoptoad, purveyor of potions,
lotions, balsams and balms, salves and
spells and ointments and charms.
Come inside, cross my palm.
It might do you good—it'll do you no harm!

Glockspindle the Magnificent. Watch him
perform the Dark Magicks from Before
the Dawn of Time! Only five sunders.
Kids half price.

Barkers and shills shouted above the general
cacophony.

"Ladeez an' genn'lemen, boyz 'n' girls! See
monsters and freaks beyond the imagination! Observe
the awesome Shellyphant, last in a line of giant clams
from the dried-up ocean bed of Rint! Converse with
the astonishing Speaking Potato of Scrunge! Marvel
at the uncanny Vegetable Lamb! Behold the terrible
Crocoduck! Dare you enter Professor Tapwindle's
Emporium of Frightfulness?"

"Aha!" Jack declared, suddenly towing Trundle off
at right angles. "Here's the very place I need!"

Trundle saw a tall gold-colored caravan with what

looked like organ pipes sticking up out of the roof. The caravan was decorated all over with musical staves and liberally sprinkled with crotchets and quavers and minims and breves and semibreves. Rollicking, rolling organ music was bellowing out of the open door. The side of the caravan had been let down and a striped awning put up, and set out on display were an astonishing array of musical instruments.

Trundle looked at a sign that hung next to the door.

Handmade Musical Instruments for Sale or Hire! Come and Test Our Wares. We have: Bladderpipes, Cornamuses, Crumhorns, Gemshorns, Hurdy-Gurdies, Psalteries, Pipes and Tabors, Racketts, Rebecs, Sackbuts, Serpents, Shawms, Viols, and Zinks. Beautiful Tones. Satisfaction Guaranteed.

Jack moved among the weird-looking musical instruments, lovingly stroking them and plucking at them and tapping them.

"I need a new rebec," he explained to Trundle.

"How can you afford to buy one?" Trundle asked.

Jack grinned. "When you spend your life on the road, you learn a trick or two," he said, stooping to remove a shoe. He gave the heel a quick twist, and a handful of gold sunders spilled into his paw. He winked at Trundle. "For emergencies."

He turned to the sales mongoose. "I'd like to try a few rebecs, please, my good fellow," he said, then turned to give Trundle another wink. "This might take a while."

"Fair enough," Trundle replied, wanting to find Esmeralda. "I'll see you later."

He left Jack with a bow in one hand and a stringed instrument in the other, his head tilted to one side as he sawed away in a flurry of merry music.

Trundle eventually came across Esmeralda chatting animatedly to an elderly beaver.

"Oh, Trundle! There you are," she said. "This is Pounceman Donk. Pounceman, this is my friend Trundle Boldoak."

Trundle solemnly shook hands with the old beaver. "Very pleased to meet you, sir."

"And you, too, young fellow my lad," said the beaver. "Esmeralda has been telling me about your intention to gather the Six Crowns of the Badger Lords." He nodded. "A noble enterprise," he said. "But one thing you should know to help you on your quest. If you walk far enough in any direction, you'll end up meeting yourself coming back again. Remember that, and you won't go far wrong."

"Oh," said Trundle. "Yes. Thank you." He glanced at Esmeralda, who was smiling behind her paw. "I'm sure that will be really helpful."

"Come on, Trundle, let's go and find Aunt Millie," Esmeralda said, pulling him away.

"What was all *that* about?" Trundle murmured once they were out of earshot.

"Oh, take no notice of Pounceman," Esmeralda said. "He's always saying stuff like that. No one knows what any of it means."

Millie Rose Thorne's caravan wasn't hard to locate. It was big and dark blue and painted with stars and moons and beaming suns. Seven steps led to the high door, over which hung an impressive sign.

Millie Rose Thorne. Queen of all the
Roamany Folk. Oracle, Diviner, Clairvoyant,
and Fortune-teller. See Your Future, for
Good or Ill, in a Reading from the Ancient
and Magical Badger Blocks!
Enter if You Dare!

A shiver ran up and down Trundle's spine as
he stood at the foot of the seven steps, each one a
different color of the rainbow. If the tingling in his
prickles was anything to go by, this caravan was simply
stiff with magic.

"Aunt Millie!" shouted Esmeralda. "Surprise! I'm
back!"

There were noises of hasty movement from
inside the caravan, and the next moment, the top
half of the door burst open and the startled face and
upper portions of a plump, elderly lady hedgehog
appeared.

"Esmeralda! Is it really you?"

Millie Rose Thorne had a blue-and-silver scarf tied around her head and huge hooped earrings hanging on either side of her round, apple-cheeked face. Her eyes widened in amazement as she stared down at Esmeralda.

"Hello, Aunty!" Esmeralda laughed, running up the steps. "I bet you didn't expect to see me again!"

"That I didn't!" gasped her aunt, flinging the bottom half of the door open. "What a resourceful child you are, to be sure!"

"You bet I am!" chuckled Esmeralda.

"And who's your little friend?" Millie Rose asked, peering down at Trundle, who was standing on the bottom step, feeling a little awkward and embarrassed and left out of it.

"He's the Lamplighter!" exclaimed Esmeralda. "Just like the Badger Blocks showed!"

"Well, well, well," said the old lady. "Come on

up, Trundle. Don't be shy. Let's make ourselves comfortable, and then you can tell me everything the two of you young folk have been up to."

Trundle scampered up the steps and followed Esmeralda and her aunt into the dark caravan. The walls were veiled in blue velvet curtains, and in the middle of the floor stood a round table with a blue cloth and a shining crystal ball. A strange, spicy scent tickled Trundle's nose and made him want to sneeze.

"Let's clear all this stuff away and have a nice cup of strawberry tea," Millie Rose said. "Do you like plum cake at all, Trundle?"

"I don't know," Trundle replied. "I've never had it."

"Never had plum cake?" exclaimed the old lady. "You poor boy! Sit ye down and make yourself comfortable while I get things organized."

Trundle sat at the table while Esmeralda's aunt whisked open the blue curtains and cleared the table. In a few moments, Trundle found himself gazing around at a lovely, homey little caravan with pink walls and windows draped with white lace, dressers filled with crockery, and a little black stove upon which a kettle was piping and steaming.

"So, children," Millie Rose said as she laid plates on the table. "Tell me all!"

"Those horrid pirates took me to Drune and sold me as a slave to work in the mines!" Esmeralda began.

"No! How very dreadful!" gasped her aunt, spooning tea into a pot.

"I'll say!" Esmeralda agreed. "But I escaped and stowed away on a windship that took me to Trundle's homeland. I knew the moment I saw him that he was the Lamplighter from the Badger Blocks! The pirates were hot on our trail by then, but we got away from them and hopped a ride on another windship that took us all the way back to Drune. And long story short—we've found the first of the crowns—the Crystal Crown! Trundle, show it to Aunt Millie."

Trundle undid the laces of his backpack and reached inside for the crown. He placed it carefully on the tablecloth. It shone and glittered in the light.

"My oh my!" said Millie Rose, her eyes gleaming. "What a very pretty thing! It must be worth a fortune!" She sat down at the table, lifting a knife and cutting thick slices from a rich, dark plum cake.

"And that's not all," said Esmeralda. "Trundle, show Aunt Millie the key."

Trundle paused with his slice of cake halfway to his mouth. He put it back on his plate and rummaged around in his backpack for the key.

He placed it on the table next to the crown.

"There!" said Esmeralda. "We found that with the crown. It has to mean something, doesn't it? It's a clue, isn't it? A clue to where the second crown can be found!"

"Well, I never," murmured her aunt, picking up the key and turning it over and over in her paws.

"Do you recognize the seals?" Trundle asked, his mouth now half full of delicious and sticky cake.

The old lady studied the seal on one side of the handle. It was an ornate letter W with vines and leaves running up and down it.

"This is the coat of arms of the ancient kings of Widdershins," she told them. She turned the key over. "I don't recognize this other seal at all, but it must have some significance."

"The second crown must be hidden in Widdershins!" cried Esmeralda. "We have to go there right now!"

"I'm sure I've heard the name Widdershins before," Trundle said. "But I don't remember anything about it."

"Well, no, my dear," Millie Rose said. "I don't imagine the simple farming folk of Shiverstones would know very much about the Guild of Observators in the ancient citadel of Widdershins."

Trundle blushed a little. "I'm afraid all we really know about is how to raise and cook cabbages," he admitted. "But I do read a lot of books," he added brightly. "And I'm . . ." His voice trailed off as an odd thought suddenly struck him. "Excuse me," he said, very politely. "But how did you know I come from Shiverstones?"

Millie Rose sipped her tea. "Oh, I'm sure you or Esmeralda must have mentioned it," she said. "Eat up your plum cake. There's plenty more."

Esmeralda was looking at her aunt with a puzzled frown on her face. "Um, actually, no," she said. "I don't think we did."

"Of course you did, my dear child," said her aunt. "Have another drop of tea, won't you?"

"Aunt Millie!" Esmeralda said, her voice suddenly rather sharp. "I am absolutely sure that neither of us mentioned Shiverstones at all." She reached across the table and drew the iron key back toward herself. "How *did* you know?"

Trundle accidentally swallowed a big chunk of plum cake.

Something was wrong here!

Very wrong indeed!

Aunt Millie Knows Best

Millie Rose Thorne sipped her tea and smiled indulgently at Esmeralda.

"You and your fancies, my dear," she chuckled. "What will you think of next?" She looked at Trundle. "More strawberry tea, Trundle?"

"Umm . . . no, thank you," mumbled Trundle.

"What's going on, Aunt Millie?" Esmeralda asked sternly. "How did you know Trundle came from Shiverstones?" She frowned at the smiling old lady. "Tell me the truth!"

"Esmeralda, Esmeralda," Millie Rose said, still smiling. "You always were such an inquisitive girl!" Her eyes twinkled. "But I suppose I ought to tell you the whole story."

"Darned right you ought!" growled Esmeralda.

"You remember that when you made that special Badger Block prophecy, your picture—the Princess in Darkness—was upside down."

"Yes, meaning problems," said Esmeralda. "So?"

"So it was hardly surprising that the pirates attacked the very next day and kidnapped you!" said her aunt. "Something like that was bound to happen. Which is why I wasn't too bothered when they popped you in a sack and made off with you."

"Thanks for your concern!" grumbled Esmeralda.

"Tush!" said her aunt. "It's not like they were going to kill you, is it? Where would be the profit in that? I knew they would sell you—and Drune is always on the lookout for healthy young slaves."

Trundle sat openmouthed, hardly able to believe his ears.

"Anyway," Aunt Millie continued. "I sent a raven messenger off to Captain Grizzletusk with a tempting offer. It got to him just after he'd sold you in the mines. The raven told him about the Badger Block prophecy, and how the blocks foretold that you would find the legendary Six Crowns of the Badger Lords of Old." She took a sip of tea. "I said I'd pay a very respectable ransom if he was prepared to follow you about on your quest until you had all six crowns. I told him you were bound to escape. And escape you did! I mean, the Fates weren't going to let you waste away in Drune after a prophecy like that!"

She chuckled. "Of course, pirates being pirates, they couldn't just quietly follow you—they simply *had* to attack Port Shiverstones!" She tutted and shook her head. "Those rascals will do anything for a quick profit!" She smiled again. "But the long and the short of it is that I've been in communication with the *Iron Pig* all along. And very satisfying it was, too, till you managed to outrun them in the Goills! I thought all my clever plans were in ruins till you turned up good as gold on my doorstep, like the precious child you are!"

"You . . . ! You . . . !" Esmeralda jumped to her feet, spilling the pink tea across the tablecloth in her rage. "You wretched excuse for an aunt!"

Trundle looked from one to the other with growing alarm.

"Calm down, Esmeralda," said her aunt. "My, but you always were such an excitable child. It all worked out for the best, didn't it? You found the crown. And you found a clue with it. Now then, sit down, my dear, and let's finish our tea like civilized people. What must our guest think of your manners?" She beamed at Trundle. "More cake, Trundle, dear?"

"No . . . thank you," mumbled Trundle. "Not . . . very . . . hungry . . . anymore . . ."

"Sit down and finish our *tea*?" hollered Esmeralda. "Not on your life! Trundle, grab the crown and the key—we're getting out of here!"

Bewildered and befuddled, Trundle snatched up the crown and key off the table and shoved them into his backpack. One thing was certain—Esmeralda's Aunt Millie was not quite the sweet old lady she seemed. Not at all, she wasn't!

Millie Rose put her cup down and stood up. "Now stop this nonsense, both of you," she said. "Or I will have to get cross with you."

"You put me in so much danger, you horrible, horrible person!" raged Esmeralda as she backed toward the door. "I never want to see you again! I hate you!"

"Tsk, tsk!" said Millie Rose, edging around the table. "What an unkind thing to say! And after I brought you up like you were my own kith and kin! But I can see you're upset." She reached out with plump, curved fingers. "Come here, my dear, and let Aunty kiss it better."

"No fear!" yelled Esmeralda, bounding backward.

Seeing a rather unpleasant light growing in the old lady's eyes, Trundle stepped in front of Esmeralda and drew his sword.

"I'm terribly sorry," he said, backing off with the point aimed at the old lady. "But I'm going to have to ask you to keep away." He hoped she wouldn't notice how much the sword was shaking in his hand. He glared indignantly at her. "I mean to say! What kind of an aunt are you, anyway? Esmeralda could have been killed any number of times over the past few days."

"What a fuss you do make!" the old lady said

kindly. "It would have been so much easier
if you'd kept your silly questions and worries to
yourself and just trusted me." She shook her
head and sighed. "But if you insist
on doing things the hard way,
well . . . so be it. I've done
my best, and no aunty
could do more."

So saying, she lifted her
hands out toward them, her chubby
fingers wriggling like worms.

"Madam, I must
warn you, if you try—"
Trundle began,
but quite suddenly
his mouth became so
dry that he could
no longer speak.
His eyes

widened as he saw long black threads of smoke emerging from Aunt Millie's fingertips. The smoke came questing through the air, undulating and slithering as the two friends backed away.

Suddenly the slinking threads of smoke darted forward and down and coiled themselves around their ankles.

"Stop doing that!" Esmeralda exclaimed, struggling to get free.

"Oh, I think not," said her aunt, her fingers still wiggling as the ropes of smoke spun out and wrapped themselves more and more tightly around Esmeralda and Trundle's ankles.

Trundle realized that his numbed feet were anchored to the floor. He could feel a bitter coldness rising up through his legs. He slashed at the sinister threads, but the blade of his sword passed right through them and they kept on coming. Even as he fought to get free, the black strands came curling and swirling up his legs, past his knees and around his waist.

"You brute!" gasped Esmeralda, fighting in vain against the paralyzing Roamany magic. "I'll pay you back for this! You see if I don't!"

"Yes, dear, of course you will," crooned her aunt. "But right now, Aunty has some business to attend to." She called out, "Bruno! Get in here! I need you!"

A few moments later, the door to the caravan opened behind them. Trundle craned his stiffening neck to see who had entered.

It was a large, muscular bear clad in a circus costume, with a rather witless expression on his face. "Yus, ma'am?" he growled in a dull, flat voice.

Millie Rose smiled kindly at Esmeralda. "Now you mustn't think for one moment that Aunty doesn't love you to pieces, my dear," she said gently. "But you always were such a . . . *scamp!* Naughty enough to break an aunty's poor soft heart, you are!" She sighed. "Bruno is going to take you both somewhere that I'm afraid you might find rather dark and dank and uncomfortable. While you're there, I'd like you to have a good long think."

"About what, exactly?" snarled Esmeralda.

"Why, about whether you're willing to help Aunty find the rest of the crowns, of course."

"Go find them yourself!" shouted Trundle. "We won't help you!"

"And that goes double for me with brass bells on!" added Esmeralda.

"Well, you see, I *would* go and find them myself," said Millie Rose. "But I can't do it without you. The prophecy of the Badger Blocks made it quite clear that the two of *you* must do the actual hunting. So you need to choose whether you'd like to find the crowns for me—or whether you'd rather wait till Captain Grizzletusk arrives to help you make up your minds."

"We left Grizzletusk on the other side of the Goills!" shouted Esmeralda. "He's whole skies away!"

"That was very resourceful of you, my dear," said her aunt. "But I asked the good captain to come straight to me if he ever lost track of you. So, you see, he's on his way here right now." She smiled, cocking her head as though listening. "Do I hear the sound of cutlasses being sharpened?" she mused. "Well, possibly. Either way, the *Iron Pig* could arrive at any moment. Won't that be a nice surprise for all these good folk?" She chuckled genially. "That would certainly put the rats in among the cheese!"

"You wicked woman!" gasped Esmeralda. "You'd set pirates on them?"

"I might have to, if you and your little friend can't be more reasonable," said Millie Rose. "The magic crowns aren't going to find *themselves*, now, are they?"

Trundle remembered all too well the ferocity of the pirate attack on his hometown of Port Shiverstones. "You couldn't be so heartless!" he gasped.

"Well, actually, Trundle, dear, I rather think I could," said the old lady. "You two go and have a good long ponder. But remember, my dears, Aunty won't take no for an answer, and if you can't make up your own minds, Grizzletusk will have to help you. Pirates can be very rough. Small things like you might easily get broken! And then where would we be?"

"I hate you!" shrieked Esmeralda.

"Oh, you're just saying that because you're cross with me," her aunt chided. "But don't worry, Aunty forgives you. Bruno! Take them and lock them in the midden trailer, there's a good chap."

"Yus, ma'am," growled the bear.

Trundle was able to twist his neck enough to see the big, burly bear looming up behind them with his great furry arms stretched out.

"I'm sorry, Trundle," Esmeralda groaned, the black coils writhing up around her neck. "I'm sorry I ever got you into this!" And then the fingers of smoke slid around her mouth, and she could say no more.

THE RAVEN
MESSENGER

Trundle fought ferociously against the smoky black coils that poured from the old lady's fingers. They were wrapped around him like freezing-cold snakes—numbing his limbs—rooting him to the spot—paralyzing him. And now they were climbing up around his neck. But all his struggles were in vain; it was impossible to get free of Millie Rose Thorne's evil spell.

Then, at the moment of final despair, Trundle

heard a small, cheerful voice pipe up from just outside the open door of the caravan.

"Hello, you people," said Jack. "Here you are at last! I've been looking all over for you!"

Trundle saw Jack's beaming face pop out from behind Bruno's great shaggy leg. "What's going on here, then?" he asked innocently. "Are we having fun and games?"

Esmeralda's aunt glared at the newcomer. "Get out of here, you vermin!" she hissed.

Jack's eyebrows shot up. "I say!" he exclaimed. "That's a bit strong, madam!"

But in that moment, while the old lady's attention was distracted, Trundle felt the black coils loosen enough for him to be able to lift his arm and to bring the flat of his sword down sharply on her wiggling fingers.

"Yow!" she shouted, snatching her hands away. "That hurt, you nasty boy!"

"Good!" Trundle declared. "Serves you right!"

"Trundle, I'm free!" yelled Esmeralda, beating at the wavering threads that wound around her. The coils were no longer black. They had become gray and pale and as insubstantial as mist.

Trundle spun around to confront Bruno. The big bear's arms were still stretched out to grab them, but he snarled and drew back as the blade whisked to and fro in front of his muzzle.

"Run for it!" Trundle yelled.

"You ain't going nowhere!" growled Bruno, lunging forward again.

"Take a bet?" yelled Esmeralda, diving between the bear's legs. She plunged headfirst through the caravan door, crashing into Jack and bowling him off his feet. They landed in a tangled heap at the foot of the steps.

"I got *you*, anyhow, you urchin!" snarled Bruno, his little eyes burning in his big face as he lurched toward Trundle.

"Urchin, indeed!" yelled Trundle, prancing to one side and poking his sword at the bear's big hairy belly. "Take that!" The thick fur blocked his thrust, but the very tip of the blade made contact with flesh. The bear let out a howl of anger and pain.

"Grab him, you dolt!" Trundle heard Millie Rose shout.

Not likely! thought Trundle.

The bear's arms swung at him like a huge pair of pincers. Trundle ducked down and rolled to the doorway. Giving Bruno a parting prod in the big toe, he flung himself out of the caravan and down the steps.

He crash-landed on Jack and Esmeralda just as they were getting up. All three sprawled breathlessly in the grass. Trundle was aware of a twanging noise from a musical instrument that was strapped to Jack's back.

There was a ferocious roar from above. Bruno's

brawny shape filled the doorway to the caravan. His eyes burned with fury, his jaws gaping, his lips drawn back to reveal rows of sharp yellow fangs.

The three companions stared up at the hideous vision for a split second. Then they were on their feet and running like crazy through the crowded Roamany fairground.

Roaring and snarling, Bruno came lumbering after them.

"This way!" panted Esmeralda as they ducked and dived among the sideshows and booths. She vaulted into a Stun-a-Stoat stall, and as the other two followed, she pulled them down under cover.

"We're not here!" she hissed to the puzzled-looking stallholder.

"Fair enough," he said, unperturbed.

Trundle heard the rapid approach of ponderous feet. There was the rasp of panting breath. "Have you scen two hedgehogs and a squirrel come this way?" growled Bruno.

"Yessir, Mr. Strongbear," said the stallholder, pointing randomly. "They went thataway!"

Bruno snarled in frustration and went careering off.

"Thanks, Tinker," Esmeralda said to the stallholder, rising and peeking over the top of the wooden barrier.

"Don't mention it, princess," said Tinker. "Glad to help."

"It's all right," Esmeralda said to her friends. "He's gone. Now let's get out of here!"

"I think . . . we're safe . . . now!" gasped Esmeralda, snatching a glance over her shoulder as they raced down Port Tentercombe High Street.

"When we get . . . a moment . . ." panted Jack, "can someone . . . please tell me . . . what's going on?"

"Horrible treachery!" said Esmeralda. "Unbelievably horrible treachery!"

"You can say that again!" added Trundle.

"We have to get off this island right now!" said Esmeralda. "Let's hope those provisions we bought have been put aboard the *Thief in the Night*— otherwise we'll have to set sail without them!" And so saying, she put on a renewed burst of speed, and the three friends went hurtling through Port Tentercombe like rockets.

They were in luck. The stern of the *Thief in the Night* was piled high with boxes and sacks and crates. The Gents' and Ladies' Outfitters had not let them down.

Esmeralda leaped into the skyboat and started unfurling the sail, while Jack and Trundle untied the mooring ropes. The *Thief in the Night* bobbed free of its moorings, and Jack and Trundle jumped aboard. Jack got busy with the rigging, and Esmeralda clambered over their provisions to get to the tiller.

The wind caught in the sail, and the skyboat rose into the air. Esmeralda turned the tiller, and the slim vessel described an elegant curve in the air, rising above Port Tentercombe.

Trundle peered down. They were sailing out over the Roamany fairground. He thought he even caught a glimpse of Millie Rose Thorne's caravan before the skyboat sailed higher in the sky and the colors merged and blurred in the green of the wide meadowlands and hills of Tenterwold.

"She's a bit sluggish," Esmeralda called to Jack. "It must be all this weight. Jack, can you set the jib sail for me? The main sail might not be enough to give us the speed we need."

"Aye, aye," said Jack, and a few minutes later, a second sail was up and filling with wind.

"That's more like it!" said Esmeralda. "Trundle, be a good fellow and have a hunt through the stuff for the sky charts we bought."

Trundle eyed the large pile of provisions. "What will they look like?" he asked.

"A metal tube with writing on it," said Esmeralda. "The charts will be rolled up inside."

Trundle began to search. It wasn't easy.

Among the equipment that Esmeralda had purchased was a barrel filled with fresh spring water, an economy-sized box of hardtack biscuits, a barrel of fresh fruit, another barrel of dried fruit, a box of salt fish, a brace of Gravelsdyke salami and a couple of wheels of very ripe Old Sox Tenterwold cheese. Also in the pile, there was a sun compass, blankets and oilskins, hurricane lamps, rope, soap, sticks, picks, a shovel, and some distress flares for just in case—oh! And right at the very bottom, in the most inaccessible place possible, the brass tube of sky charts!

Trundle struggled to free himself from the pile of provisions, clutching the tube in triumph as he emerged.

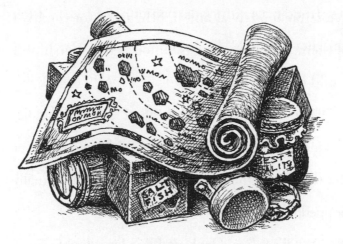

"Good lad," said Esmeralda. "Now, find me the chart with Widdershins on it."

Jack raised an eyebrow. "We're going to Widdershins, are we?" he asked.

"We are," said Trundle, wrestling to get the tube open.

"Well, well," mused Jack.

"Have you been there before?" asked Esmeralda.

"Not at all," said Jack, shaking his head. "Quite the reverse, in fact. They don't like musicians and entertainers there, no, sir, they certainly don't.

We're far too trivial and lighthearted for the likes of them. They're a serious bunch at the Worshipful Guild of Observators."

"The worshipful *who* of *what?*" asked Trundle, picking up the charts that had scattered all over the bottom of the skyboat when the top had finally popped off the tube.

"You'll see," said Jack, nodding knowingly.

"Trundle!" There was a sudden urgency in Esmeralda's voice. "You've got good eyes. What's that coming up behind us?"

Trundle's heart leaped up into his throat. He peered back the way they had come. Tenterwold was now just a greenish pebble in the distance—but shooting swift as an arrow from that same direction came a small black shape.

"It's a bird," Jack said, shading his eyes.

"A big bird," agreed Trundle. "A big black bird."

The shape grew as it drew closer.

"It's a raven!" gasped Jack. "Gosh! And a right big one, too!"

As the black bird came closer, it rose high above them, soaring through the air with fast-beating wings. They stared up as it passed over them. Trundle could have sworn that a beady red eye peered malevolently down at them.

"Is it Captain Slaughter? Razorback's bird?" he asked in a trembling voice, remembering the wicked raven companion to the pirate bosun of the *Iron Pig*.

"I don't think so," said Esmeralda.

"Thank heavens!" gasped Trundle.

"Don't be so very thankful just yet," warned Esmeralda. "Don't forget, my aunt uses ravens as messengers—and that raven is heading the same way we are."

Jack looked hollowly at them. "Meaning it will be in Widdershins ahead of us," he said. "I don't like the idea of that."

"Neither do I," said Esmeralda, her face becoming grim. "I think we're going to have to be very careful when we come to the Worshipful Guild of Observators," she added ominously. "Very careful indeed!"

The Worshipful Guild of Observators

"So," asked Trundle as the *Thief in the Night* sailed into the glowing twilight of a warm summer evening, "what exactly is this guild of observers thing?" He took a bite of salami and looked enquiringly from Jack to Esmeralda.

"Observa-*tors*," corrected Esmeralda. "Jack, pass me the honeypot."

The tiller had been tied to keep them on course, and the three companions were sitting at their ease in the bows, having supper.

"The Guild of Observators are scientists," Esmeralda explained. "They took over the palace of the ancient kings of Widdershins hundreds and hundreds of years ago, when the royal line died out."

"And they've been there ever since," added Jack. "Thinking important thoughts and scribbling important things in their books and constructing strange and wonderful devices and machines and mapping and plotting and charting and measuring everything." He shook his head. "It's a terrible lot of knowledge they have. It makes my head ache just to think of it."

"The charts we're using were plotted by the guild," Esmeralda explained to Trundle. "They're clever like that." She spread honey on a slice of bread. "But," she added with a rather self-satisfied smile, "they don't have any magic. Only us Roamanys have *magic*."

Mention of the Roamanys made Trundle uneasy. "What do you think your aunt is going to do now? She knows where we're going—and she knows why." His forehead wrinkled. "And what do you think that raven was sent to do?"

"To spy on us once we get to Widdershins, I suppose," said Esmeralda. "We'll need to keep our eyes open—and kill it if we get the chance!"

Trundle looked unhappily at her. He didn't like the sound of *killing* at all. "I suppose she'll send the pirates after us again," he said.

"If she does, we'll, outrun 'em," Esmeralda declared. "The *Thief in the Night* is the fastest skyboat in the seven hundred skies of the Sundered Lands!" She smiled confidently at him. "Besides, I don't care if every pirate in creation chases after us. This is our quest, and we're going to see it through."

"Good for you, Esmeralda!" cried Jack. "Three cheers for us! And when we're done, I shall write an epic ballad about our adventures." He reached for his brand-new rebec and bow and, sawing away on the strings, he began tentatively to sing. "*Two hedgehogs and a squirrel bold . . . tumty-tumty . . . crowns of old . . . They sailed across the azure sky . . .*"

"And ended up left in a ditch to die," murmured Trundle.

Jack laughed and slapped him heartily on the back. "That won't do at all!" he said. "It doesn't even scan properly. No, no! What rhymes with sky? Fly, sigh, fry, try. That's it!" He started bowing again. "*They sailed across the azure sky, their fortune and their fate to try!* This is going to be great. I need to write it down."

Trundle sighed as he handed over a pencil and some paper. Look on the bright side, he told himself. In years to come, people might sit around the fire and sing "The Ballad of the Grisly Death of Trundle Boldoak at the Hands of Evil Pirates and a Wicked Roamany Aunty."

It would be nice to be famous.

He sighed again. It would be even nicer to be alive and safe at home!

"Impressive, eh?" said Jack.

Trundle nodded. Jack was right. This was very impressive indeed.

It was a bright new morning, and the *Thief in the Night* was hanging with tethered sails above the island of Widdershins. Except, as Trundle could clearly see, Widdershins was not just *one* island—it was a collection of dozens and dozens of islands, some as big as towns, others only large enough to hold one or two buildings. The floating islands were held together by arched wooden bridges and by iron walkways and chain-link catwalks and ropewalks and overpasses. Spires and belfries and towers and steeples thrust up into the sky. Narrow tip-tilted streets and stairways wound up and down and in and out of the tightly packed buildings. People in hooded habits scuttled about as though intent on important business.

But as Trundle gazed down in awe, his eyes were drawn irresistibly to the huge island that formed the heart of the age-old city. It rose up above all the other islands like a mountain, steep sided, craggy, and rugged. Here and there, windswept trees and bushes pushed out from between the buildings that clung to its sheer sides like limpets to a rock. Up and up it soared to a great palace of rearing walls and time-worn battlements and keeps and halls and towers and turrets, topped off by an ornamented citadel from the apex of which rose a lofty steeple of gold that flashed in the sunlight.

"And that, my friend," said Esmeralda, "is where the Guild of Observators hangs out."

"It's amazing," breathed Trundle. "I've never seen anything like it."

"Face it, Trundle," said Esmeralda. "Before you

met me you'd never seen anything, period!"

"Except cabbages," added Jack with a wide smile.

"Yes," Trundle agreed, turning away from the awesome sight. "Many a cabbage. So what's the plan? What do we do now?"

"We make landfall and go chat with the big boss," said Esmeralda. "We'll show him the crown and the key. He's bound to know what the key is for. I'm betting it fits a big golden chest that will have the Iron Crown sitting inside it on a purple velvet cushion."

Jack shook his head. "My guess is it'll be the key to a long-forgotten room at the top of a deserted tower." His voice lowered. "We'll open the door and we'll find a throne all covered in spiders' webs . . . and sitting on the throne will be a skeleton dressed in rotting rags—the skeleton of the last king of Widdershins. And the Iron Crown will still be on his fleshless, hollow-eyed skull. And when we try to take it, the dead king will speak, putting a terrible curse on us." Jack laughed. "That'll be exciting, won't it?"

"That's all we need," said Trundle. "To be cursed!"

"No one's getting cursed," said Esmeralda. "Come on, you two. Let's get busy. And remember, keep your eyes peeled for any ravens. Aunt Millie's messenger could be here already, and we don't want to be taken by surprise."

Mooring the *Thief in the Night* on an outer island, they made their way through the maze of old streets, across rickety bridges, up narrow twisting stairways, along deep-set alleys and passages, heading always inward and upward.

Trundle found Widdershins even more imposing and grand from close up, but he began to notice something else as well. The whole place was falling to pieces. Here and there, entire buildings had collapsed into rubble, and many another old edifice was being propped up by wooden scaffolding or held together by great iron staples or by loops of thick, tarred rope.

Widdershins was still awesome, but Trundle began to find it a little sad as well.

At last they found themselves standing on a wide cobbled courtyard in front of massive wooden gates, gazing up at writing etched into the gray stone and picked out in faded gold leaf.

COLLEGE OF
THE WORSHIPFUL
GUILD OF OBSERVATORS
HIGHMOST CHANCELLOR:
AUGUSTUS BROCKWISE,
M.SC. M.PHIL. M.ENG. PH.D.

Nailed to the doorpost, alongside a hanging chain, was a scrap of parchment.

For admittance, pull chain once and WAIT.
A guard will come.

And underneath that, a scribbled note.

Don't pull more than once, or you'll be in for it!

Esmeralda marched up to the bell pull and gave it a hefty tug. A gloomy bell rang dully from behind the walls.

They waited.

Esmeralda folded her arms and leaned against the wall. Trundle walked nervously up and down, the backpack containing the crown and the key slung over his shoulder. Jack shoved his hands in his pockets and whistled cheerily to himself.

Nothing happened.

Esmeralda stood and stared at the bell pull, her fists on her hips. "If they don't answer the door by the time I count to ten . . . ," she began, but she was interrupted by a small side door creaking open.

A sleepy-eyed fox in an elaborate but shoddy uniform stepped out. He had a dented crested helmet on his head and a slightly bent halberd in one fist. He blinked at the three companions and wiped a sleeve across his nose.

"Whaddya want?" he asked.

"My name is Esmeralda Lightfoot," announced Esmeralda. "And these are my trusted companions, Trundle Boldoak and Jack Nimble. We have urgent business to discuss with the Highmost Chancellor, so be a good fellow and let us in."

"Wot biznizz?" asked the guard, frowning down at her.

"That's our affair," Esmeralda declared. "Kindly alert your master to our presence."

"No tell me biznizz, no geddin," mumbled the guard, turning and ducking back through the little postern door.

"Now look here, you!" exclaimed Esmeralda.

The guard turned and regarded her with narrowed eyes. "Wot?"

Trundle had the feeling that Esmeralda's temper was likely to do more harm than good. He stepped forward, pulling the Crystal Crown and the iron key out of the backpack.

"Look!" he said to the guard. "We've found these! We want to show them to the Highmost Chancellor. I'm sure he'll be interested."

The guard peered at him. "Wossis, then?"

"It's the Crystal Crown of the Badger Lords of Old," said Jack. "We're on a quest to find all of them. We're hoping the Highmost Chancellor will be able to help."

"I'll arx 'im," mumbled the guard, and before Trundle or Jack or Esmeralda could say a word or make a move or do anything to prevent it, he leaned forward, grabbed the crown and the key out of Trundle's hands, and disappeared back through the doorway.

"Come back in six weeks," the guard said. "Maybe someone'll see you then."

The door slammed shut on them.

"Hey!" they yelled in chorus. "Wait!"

They threw themselves at the door and hammered on it till their paws were bruised and aching.

But despite their very best efforts, the door remained firmly shut.

6

OVER THE ROOFTOPS

The three companions sat dejectedly under the high stone walls of the Worshipful Guild of Observators, robbed of crown and key and wondering what to do next.

No amount of hammering and yelling had made the guard open the door again. At one point Esmeralda had taken off her shoe and beaten it on the great oak wood panels for a solid minute, but to no effect.

"I suppose we *could* come back again in six weeks' time, like he said," mused Trundle, his chin in his paws and his spirits in his heels.

"Good plan, Trundle," Esmeralda replied with deep sarcasm. "And by then, of course, the pirates will be here to help us out."

"I was only *saying* . . . ," mumbled Trundle.

"If we had a rope and a grappling hook, we might be able to scale the walls," said Jack.

"The rope back on the *Thief in the Night* isn't long enough," said Esmeralda. "And we don't have a grappling hook."

"I once heard of a fellow who escaped from prison by tunneling right under the walls," Jack offered. "He did it with a spoon and a fork. He was a steam mole, by the name of Edwin Tilthammer. Got locked up for counterfeiting gold sunders. The tunnel took him—oh!" Jack frowned. "I'll shut up now."

Trundle looked sideways at him. "The tunnel took him . . . ?"

"Two and a half years," muttered Jack. "Sorry. Not helpful." He gave a plucky smile. "I could cheer us up by singing an old chain-gang ditty I picked up in Wetwhistle one time."

"Not if I sit on your head, you couldn't," growled Esmeralda. She looked at Trundle. "How could you have just handed the crown and the key over to him like that?"

"I didn't hand them over," Trundle protested. "He took them."

"He wouldn't have *took* them from me!"

"Well, if you're so clever—"

"Chaps, chaps!" interrupted Jack. "Arguing won't get us anywhere." He stood up. "Positive action is what's required now, and lots of it."

He looked down at the gloomy hedgehogs for a few moments, then turned on his heel and went striding along the wall. Whistling gaily to himself, he vanished around a corner.

Trundle glanced at Esmeralda. "I'm sorry," he said. "You trusted me with the crown and the key, and I totally let you down."

"Oh, it wasn't your fault," said Esmeralda. "Who knew *that* was going to happen?"

There was a short silence before Trundle spoke again. "And I'm sorry that your aunty turned out to be such a . . . such a . . ."

"Pig-dog-rat-fink-skunk-monster from Boweldeeps?" Esmeralda finished. "Yes, so am I." She shook her head. "I can't believe that she's in cahoots with Grizzletusk." She looked at Trundle. "I don't even want to *think* about what would happen if those pirates ever got their hands on the Six Crowns."

"'What *would* happen?" Trundle asked. "Didn't I just tell you I don't want to think about it?"

"Yes, but . . . well, I know the rhyme—'*if power ye*

seek,' and all that. But exactly what kind of power do the crowns have? What would happen if they were all gathered together?"

"No one knows," Esmeralda replied. "That's what's so scary. The last time the Six Crowns were all in one place, the whole world blew up! Aunt Millie seems to think Grizzletusk will just meekly hand the crowns over to her if she pays him enough—but I seriously doubt it. I think he'll keep the crowns for himself." She gave him a bleak look. "Would you want a source of power like that to fall into the hands of *pirates*?"

"No, not much," Trundle said miserably.

Just then, Jack came pattering back, grinning from ear to ear. "Come with me," he said. "I've got a plan."

They got up and followed him to the corner of the wall. At the point where the wall turned, it began a steep climb up the natural rock of the cone-shaped island. Walls and battlements and towers climbed up and up above them across a cracked rock face studded vith gnarled and twisted trees and barbed with thorny bushes. Jack pointed up through the branches of a straggly hawthorn. "See that scaffolding?" he said. Trundle saw it—a construction of wooden beams and planks and poles pressing up against the walls about sixty feet above their heads.

"That's our way in," said Jack. "Up the scaffolding and over the walls. What do you say?"

"I say, 'Well done, Jack,'" said Esmeralda.

And so they began the long, steep climb up to the scaffolding. Jack went first, scouting out the easiest route and helping them when they got stuck.

It was hard going, and Trundle was soon puffing and blowing as he heaved himself up the knuckled fists of rock. He paused, panting. Jack peered at him, grinning as usual. "Come on, stumpy legs," he said, reaching down a helpful paw. "We're almost there."

"I happen to have rather elegant legs," Trundle gasped, "for a hedgehog."

"Good for you," laughed Jack.

"Get a move on!" panted Esmeralda, from beneath.

Trundle made a final effort, and soon the three of them were standing directly under the scaffolding. They could see why it was needed—a great crumbling crack ran down the length of the wall, and part of the stonework was bulging out in a very precarious manner. Unfortunately, the zigzagging crack wasn't wide enough to climb through.

"This scaffold looks like it's been here for years," Esmeralda said, eyeing the network of poles and beams and spars and timbers. "Do you think it's safe?"

"Of course it is," said Jack. "Watch!" He spat on his paws and then went scurrying up the scaffolding while Esmeralda and Trundle watched from below.

Jack's head bobbed out from the top of the scaffolding. "As easy as that!" he called down.

The two hedgehogs looked at each other.

"Here goes nothing," said Trundle, reaching for the first beam.

It was a nerve-wracking and a tricky and an awkward climb, but Jack was always there to help out when things got really difficult, and it was not too long before Trundle and Esmeralda were standing on the lofty and creaking summit of the scaffold.

"It's probably not a good idea to look down if you're not used to heights," Jack warned them.

"Don't worry, I wasn't going to!" said Esmeralda.

Moving slowly, and clinging on with both hands whenever possible, the two hedgehogs followed

Jack across the scaffolding
and onto the top of the wall.
Then they jumped down
onto a narrow walkway.

Curiosity overcoming
his fear, Trundle peered
down. Far below, he
saw cloisters and
courtyards and
quadrangles linked
by pathways that
wound between the
tall, heavily ornamented
buildings. Even in their
slow decay, the buildings
were magnificent and
breathtaking, with their
tall arched windows
of colored glass

and their pillars and pediments, their sculpted architraves and cornices, and their rooftop gargoyles and statues.

And even at this height, the taller towers and steeples surged up above them like ornate stalagmites, topped with stone-carved stars and suns and crescent moons.

Staring up at the timeless hugeness of it all, Trundle suddenly felt dreadfully small and unimportant.

"Oi! What are you doing up here?"

Trundle's thoughts were disturbed by the sound of a rough voice. A badger in workman's clothes and a cloth cap, holding a bricklayer's hod, was staring at them from farther along the wall.

"Run!" said Esmeralda.

They ran, pursued by the steady clomping of hobnailed boots and by gruff shouts. "Come back here! I'll report you!"

The precarious walkway led them to a narrow flight of stone steps that disappeared into a small opening in a round turret. They plunged headlong into the turret and raced up a spiral stairway. It led them to a flat rooftop encircled by low battlements. They ran from side to side. There was no obvious way down. They could hear the echoing thud of the workman's boots coming up the stairs.

Jack pointed across to a nearby rooftop of copper sheets, green with verdigris. "We can jump," he said.

"Never," gasped Trundle, staring down into the long drop between.

"Easy as pie!" said Jack. He climbed up onto the battlements, paused for a few moments, then jumped. He handed light-footedly on the other side.

Esmeralda and Trundle hesitated. That kind of thing was easy enough for a squirrel! They didn't have much time to make up their minds; the irate badger was almost upon them.

They clasped hands and stepped up onto the battlements.

"On three," said Esmeralda.

Trundle nodded, too terrified to speak.

"One . . . two . . . *three!*"

And with that, they launched themselves headlong off the battlements.

7

TRUNDLE THE BRAVE!

Trundle's stomach turned over several times as he and Esmeralda flew hand in hand through the air. The impossible gulf yawned under his feet. Then there was a crash and a thud as they landed safely on the copper roof.

"Phew!" gasped Esmeralda. "Who knew hedgehogs could fly?"

Following Jack, they tottered along the sloping roof until they came to a small dormer window. Jack quickly had the window open, and in a few moments they were all standing together on the bare and dusty wooden floorboards of a deserted attic room.

"We're in!" panted Esmeralda.

"That we are," said Jack. "Neat as you like!"

"Now what?" asked Trundle.

"Now we go get the crown and the key back!" said Esmeralda, heading for the door.

The long wood-paneled corridor was quite empty. Sunlight slanted in through mullioned windows, picking out old oil paintings of elderly, severe-looking badgers in dark robes. There were many doors. All of them were closed.

"All clear," whispered Trundle, creeping down the last couple of steps of the attic stairway. Esmeralda and Jack emerged with him into the long, silent corridor.

"So far, so good," said Jack, peering up at a suit of

armor that stood glowering in a corner. "Nice-looking fellow," he said, eyeing the double-edged battle-ax held between the gauntlets.

There was a muffled sound of movement from somewhere close by. Trundle saw a door handle turning.

"Get back!" he hissed. Esmeralda and Jack scrambled back up the stairs, and Trundle ducked behind the suit of armor.

The door opened. Peeping from between the leg armor, Trundle saw a bespectacled old badger in long purple robes come sweeping into the corridor. He was followed by a scuttling line of hedgehogs and voles and squirrels, all dressed in brown habits, and all tottering under the weight of scrolls and parchments and books and folders.

As he swept majestically along, Trundle could hear the elderly badger talking rapidly to himself.

". . . with no equator, save that which can be

extrapolated from the relative positions of the islands *in situ* and calculated as an empirical mathematical inevitability, using the explosion as point zero, how do we now utilize the meta-planispheric astrolabe without taking into account the effects of the gravitational pull of both the sun itself and those higher bodies in the Sundered Lands which, it must be admitted . . ."

As he passed along the corridor, the patter of two dozen following feet drowned out his voice. Blinking, Trundle watched them trail off into the distance. A few moments more, and the corridor was empty and quiet again.

Trundle stepped out of hiding as Esmeralda and Jack came back down the stairs.

"Did you hear him?" asked Trundle, wide-eyed. "I didn't understand a word he was saying! He must be such a brainbox!"

Esmeralda raised an eyebrow. "That's what they'd

like everyone to think," she said. "If you ask me, all that science talk is a lot of blather and waffle."

Jack looked thoughtful. "If we were dressed up in brown robes like those chaps following the badger, we'd be able to get around here without making people suspicious," he said.

"Good thinking," said Esmeralda. "Let's keep our eyes peeled for a cloakroom or a store cupboard."

Luck was with them. They had only gone down two flights of stairs and along three corridors before they spotted a pair of squirrels pushing a trolley filled with crumpled brown habits.

"Laundry basket!" whispered Esmeralda, following at a safe distance.

The trolley was pushed into a deserted washing room, and the two squirrels scuttled off. A few minutes later, the three companions were wrapped up in the cleanest of the brown habits from the laundry. Thus disguised, they found that they were

able to walk quite freely through the halls and corridors without anyone paying them any attention.

There were plenty of people about—scores of small animals in brown habits swarmed around the hallways, sometimes bearing armfuls of books and scrolls, sometimes hauling trolleys along behind them, the wheels creaking under the weight of musty old books.

Every now and then they would pass a room with an open door. Trundle found these rooms fascinating. Some were like classrooms, every desk occupied by badgers paying earnest attention to teachers who scribbled complex equations on big blackboards. Other rooms were filled with strange machinery that whirred and chimed and clicked and spun while badgers moved around taking notes or making adjustments or rubbing their wise chins and looking thoughtful.

There were signs at every turn and junction in the maze of corridors, pointing to the Orrery Chamber, or the Torquetum or the Astrarium or the Gymbelorium.

And many of the doors had brass plates attached, such as Professor Erasmus Quiverwhisker: Advanced Theories in Circular Diminishment or Dr. Jervays Hardclaw: Ponderology and Imponderology.

Slowly they wound their way down and down until they came upon a sign that read Entrance Lobby, Visitors' Waiting Room, Outer Bailey, Guardhouse, Main Gate, and Exit.

"What if the guard recognizes us?" Trundle asked as they walked across the cobbled courtyard toward the great wooden gates and the small stone guardhouse that stood to one side.

"So long as we keep our hoods up, he won't see our faces," Esmeralda said. She looked from Jack to Trundle. "Now, remember—we've been sent by Doctor Hardclaw to collect the crown and the key so they can be studied."

"Got it," said Jack, only his nose visible under the hood.

"Check," added Trundle, pulling his hood deeper over his face.

The guardhouse door was wide open, revealing a small chamber with a desk and a chair and with various racks and notice boards attached to the walls. The guard was leaning back on two legs of the chair, his feet up on the desk and his nose in a newspaper.

Esmeralda rapped on the door. "Excuse me!" she said in an authoritative voice. "We're here to collect the crown and the key."

The guard turned his head and eyed her without interest. All the same, Trundle pulled his hood a little farther forward as the three of them stepped into the room.

"Izzat so?" said the guard. "Oo wants 'em?"

"Doctor Hardclaw," said Esmeralda. "He needs them urgently, so be a good fellow and hand them over."

The guard leaned down behind his desk and pulled out the crown and the key. Trundle could hardly believe how smoothly things were going. Their plan was really going to work!

Esmeralda took the two precious objects from the guard's big, clumsy paws.

"Thank you," she said. "Sorry to disturb you."

The guard snorted and picked up his newspaper.

Esmeralda turned and headed for the doorway. Trundle did likewise, with Jack close behind. But just as they were about to exit, Trundle felt something come down hard on the hem of his robes, bringing him to a jerking halt and yanking the hood back off his head.

"Oops, sorry," said Jack. "Excuse my big feet!"

The guard turned and peered at Trundle's suddenly revealed face.

"Here! I know you!" he growled. "You're the

bloke wot woz outside not two hours since! How'd you get in?" He lurched forward. "Gimme them things back! You ain't from Doc Hardclaw at all, I'll warrant. You're interlopers and trespassers."

So saying, he leaped up, and with one hand he slammed the door shut in Esmeralda's face, while with the other he reached for his halberd.

Reacting in an instant, Esmeralda spun around and kicked the guard's shins.

"Yowp!" howled the guard, almost dropping his halberd.

A moment later, Jack jumped up onto the desk, swiping up anything he could lay paws on and flinging it at the guard's head. And while all this was going on, Trundle was struggling to get his sword out from under his habit.

"Take that!" howled Esmeralda, swinging the crown in both hands and bringing it into sharp contact with the guard's midriff.

"Oof!" gasped the guard, doubling over as Jack brought a tin mug down on his head.

But the guard wasn't so easily dealt with. He swiped a long swipe with the halberd. The sharp edge only missed Jack by a hairs breadth as he leaped for his life off the desk. The other end of the halberd caught Esmeralda behind the ear and sent her sprawling, the crown and key skittering across the floor, between the guard's legs and out of sight under the desk.

"Now I gotcha!" snarled the guard, his teeth bared as he stooped over the sprawling Esmeralda. "Mincemeat, you're gonna be!"

At that moment, Trundle finally got his sword free. Without pausing to think, he leaped between the guard and Esmeralda, determined to protect her. He held his sword out in both hands as the guard loomed over him. The look on the guard's face was so ferocious that he backed away, the sword quivering in his grip.

At that moment he was aware of a large brown

shape leaping through the air. It was Jack. With a skirling cry, he launched himself onto the guard's back. The guard tottered forward, trying vainly to pull Jack off his neck.

In all honesty, Trundle could not really have explained in detail what happened next. One moment he was waving his sword in the air, and the next moment, the guard came plunging toward him like a felled tree.

There was a dull *bonk!* as the flat edge of the sword whacked the guard a good one on the side of the head. And then, quite suddenly, Trundle was flat on his back and covered all over in heavy, limp guard.

"Gurrg," he gasped, the breath quite beaten out of him. "Get him off!"

Esmeralda and Jack dragged the unconscious guard off, and Trundle sat up, spluttering and befuddled. "What happened?" he gasped, gazing anxiously at Jack. "Did I kill him?"

"Hardly!" said Jack. "But you did manage to knock him out."

"But for how long?" wondered Esmeralda, peering into the guard's face. "I think we should tie him up— just to be on the safe side." She turned, her eyes shining. "Well done, my brave and dashing Trundle! I never thought you had it in you."

Trundle got dizzily to his feet. "I didn't . . . it wasn't . . ." He looked at the guard, a feeling of pride growing in him. "Serves him right!" he declared. "What can we tie him up with?"

"With his own trousers, what else!" laughed Jack, already loosening the limp guard's belt. "Come on, you two—help a chap out!"

In next to no time they had whipped off the guard's pants, leaving him in rather grubby knee-length underwear with frayed ends and burst seams. He was tossed unceremoniously onto his front, and the legs of his trousers were looped around and around his wrists and knotted tightly.

Esmeralda then peeled off his long socks and tied one expertly around his ankles. Finally, she lifted his head and stuffed the other sock into his mouth. "In case he wakes up and feels like shouting for help," she remarked heartlessly.

Trundle's forehead wrinkled. "All the same," he said. "Putting stinky socks in a person's mouth is a bit much, don't you think?"

Esmeralda eyed him. "He was going to chop us into tiny pieces, Trundle," she said, patting him on the back. "I think a mouthful of old sock is the least he deserves!"

Trundle picked up his sword from the floor. It felt different in his paw now—it felt suddenly very serious and important and . . . *fateful*. It had knocked out the guard and probably saved them all.

"He was going to kill us, wasn't he?" Trundle said, slipping the sword into his belt. "And I stopped him!"

"He certainly was, and you certainly did," replied Esmeralda, crawling under the desk to retrieve the crown and the key.

"You're a hero, Trundle!" said Jack.

"And now let's get out of here before someone finds us," said Esmeralda, tucking crown and key in among the folds of her robes.

They departed, and for the first time, Trundle felt as though he really was *meant* to have the sword!

8

The Highmost Chancellor Takes a Nap

There was a key in the lock on the inside of the guardhouse door. Esmeralda took it out as they left and locked the door behind them. She lifted a cobblestone and placed the key under it while Jack and Trundle kept anxious watch.

"That should give us some time before he's found," Esmeralda said, stamping the cobblestone down again.

They made their way back across the courtyard

and through an arched doorway into a wide oak-paneled vestibule, hung with the ancient banners of the guilds. A huge notice board displayed the names of every department and division and doctorate and seminary, set alongside a marquetry map of where everything could be found.

"Doctor Augustus Brockwise," Esmeralda read. "Tower of the Brazen Finials, fifth floor, room 1720."

Jack perused the map. "Got it!" he said, pointing. "We're in luck. *This* is the Tower of the Brazen *Wotsits*, and by the looks of it, the quickest way to Brockwise's lair is up those stairs over there." He pointed over to an elaborate staircase at the far end of the vestibule.

"Excellent," said Esmeralda. "And remember, we're just three ordinary workers going about our everyday business, so try to look like we belong here."

They encountered any number of magisterial badgers and scuttling minions on the way, but no one took any notice of them, and they eventually found themselves outside a large and magnificent oak door. A brass plaque confirmed they had reached their target.

OFFICE OF THE HIGHMOST CHANCELLOR, PLENIPOTENTIARY, BAGERIUS MAXIMUS BONCIUS, DOCTOR AUGUSTUS BROCKWISE

And below, a smaller notice was pinned to the panels:

Do Not Disturb

Esmeralda stepped up to the door and rapped sharply on it.

They waited for a reply.

"Maybe he's gone out?" suggested Trundle.

Esmeralda knocked again and turned the large

brass handle. The door opened with a long-drawn creak of protest.

"Hello?" she called, poking her head around the door. "Anyone—oh!" She pushed the door wider, revealing to Trundle's and Jack's eyes a room as long and as lofty as a cathedral. A purple carpet ran the length of the floor, and at the far end—about three hundred feet away—they could just make out a big, dark desk in front of a tall black chair in which someone was seated.

Even more remarkable to the friends than the size of the room were the extraordinary apparatuses and machines and devices and contraptions that lined the walls. They walked along the carpet in subdued awe, the brass and copper and steel and glass mechanisms towering above them; some with swinging pendulums, other with flickering dials or with whirring flywheels and ticking cogs and revolving escapements like the workings of great watches or clocks.

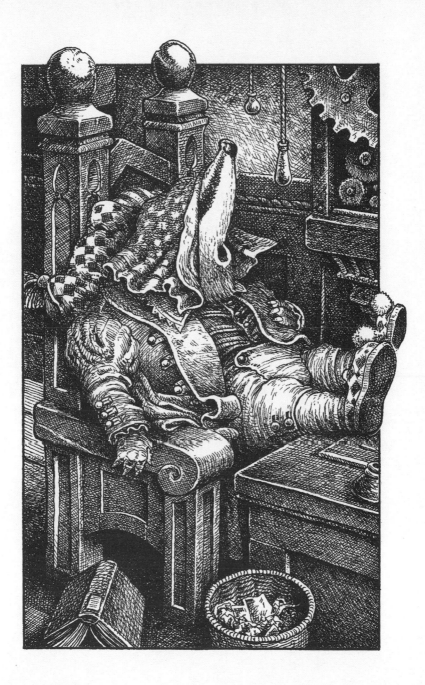

As they approached the desk, they became aware of a new sound—a grumbling, grating noise like distant thunder mixed up with someone sawing wood.

"He's asleep!" exclaimed Jack.

He was right. Slumped backward in the big black leather chair behind the desk, a portly badger snored away with his face hidden beneath a red silk handkerchief. The handkerchief fluttered and flopped with his breathing.

Apart from a blotter and an inkwell and a pen in its stand, the huge polished desk was entirely clear.

The three friends walked around the desk and stared at the slumbering Highmost Chancellor. He was wrapped in black robes, and there were carpet slippers on his feet, with red pom-poms on the toes.

"What should we do?" whispered Trundle, remembering the sign on the door and not wishing to ignore its instructions.

"Disturb him!" declared Esmeralda. She tugged at the badger's sleeve. "Hey! Excuse me!" she shouted into his hairy ear. "Wake up, please."

The badger spluttered and puffed as Esmeralda pulled off the handkerchief, revealing a wrinkled old face topped off with a pair of gold rimmed pince-nez spectacles, set slightly awry on the grizzled muzzle.

"Upon my word!" gasped the Highmost Chancellor, struggling to sit up and free his arms from the windings of his robes. "What effrontery is this?" He straightened his pince-nez and peered down at the three friends with a gimlet eye and a wrathful brow.

"Hello there," Jack said, beaming at the elderly chancellor. "Sorry we woke you up, and all."

The badger stared at them. "How dare you disturb me!" he blustered. "What effrontery! What unparalleled temerity! What unprecedented audacity—to accost your chancellor in this manner!"

"Calm down," said Esmeralda. "We only want to talk to you."

"It's worth it, honestly it is," added Trundle in a placatory voice. "We've got some things to show you."

"Recognize these?" Esmeralda asked, brandishing the crown and the key under the Highmost Chancellor's nose.

"Remove those gewgaws from my sight!" demanded the Highmost Chancellor. "Leave this room at once or I shall summon the guards!"

"Keep your wig on," said Esmeralda. "Don't you know what this is?" She flaunted the crown in front of his eyes. "It's the Crystal Crown of the Badger Lords of Old, that's what it is!"

The badger goggled at the glittering crown for a moment or two. "Preposterous!" he said. "Ridiculous!" he added. "Outrageous and ludicrous!" he concluded.

"But it is," said Jack. "Honestly, it is."

"You insensate and absurd creatures," boomed the old badger. "It's a scientifically proven fact that the Six Crowns of the Badger Lords do not exist!" He reached for a bell pull and gave it a series of fierce tugs. "I have summoned the guards," he told them. "Leave my office this instant, or I will have you forcibly removed!"

"But it's the Crystal Crown!" raged Esmeralda, almost dancing with frustration. "We found it in the mines of Drune! And this key was with it."

"It's true," said Trundle. "The magical Badger Blocks led us to it."

"Magic!" hooted the Highmost Chancellor, rising from his chair, his eyes flashing angrily. "You are Roamany scoundrels and magicians!" He groped by his chair and brought out a black lacquered walking cane. "I'll harbor no conjurers and sorcerers here!" he roared, swiping at them with the cane. "Be gone, I say!"

Trundle and Esmeralda and Jack hopped

backward around the desk to avoid the lashing cane. The badger followed them, and they retreated down the long carpet with him lumbering in hot and furious pursuit, his cane rising and falling, his face red with wrath and his black robes billowing.

"You silly old fool!" yelled Esmeralda. "Stop that for a second and let us explain!"

"I don't think he's going to listen," said Jack, ducking as a particularly close swipe whistled above his ears.

"Outrageous!" bellowed the Highmost Chancellor, chasing them with surprising speed as they raced for the door. "Roamanys in my office! Monstrous, I say! Disgraceful! Scandalous!"

They came tumbling out into the corridor with the enraged old badger hot on their heels. But his wind was all but used up by now; he leaned heavily on the door frame, swiping feebly at them, gasping and panting and mopping his face with the handkerchief.

"Are you quite done trying to bash us?" said Esmeralda, glaring up at him. "Because if you are, I'd like to get a few words in edgewise!"

The rumble of many running feet sounded from around a bend in the corridor.

"The guards!" gasped Jack.

"We have to go!" said Trundle, grabbing Esmeralda's arm.

"I'll be back!" she shouted at the Highmost Chancellor as Jack and Trundle dragged her away. "Don't you worry—I'm not done with you yet!"

At a junction in the corridor, they risked a quick look back. A posse of six or seven uniformed foxes was thundering toward them, all of them wielding halberds.

"Lawks!" said Jack. "We need to hide before that lot gets us!"

"Hide where?" groaned Trundle.

"In here!" said an unfamiliar voice at their

backs. Around the corner and out of sight of the approaching guards, a door was being held open for them. "Quickly, quickly," said the urgent but friendly voice. "Get under cover before they spot you."

Without further ado, the three friends bundled in through the open doorway, to find themselves in a large office lined with heavy wooden shelves packed solid with scrolls and tomes and documents and folders. The door snapped shut behind them.

A hedgehog in sky blue robes put his finger to his lips. "Shhh!" he said, turning a key in the lock. He pressed his ear against the door, smiling as he listened to the percussion of passing feet.

"There," he said, dusting his paws together. "I never did like those guards, noisy, brutal, dim-witted creatures that they are." He smiled genially at the three friends. "Now then," he continued. "Allow me to introduce myself, my young friends. I am the

Herald Pursuivant, Keeper
of Scrolls, and Personal
Secretary to His Nibs
the Highmost
Chancellor of the
Worshipful Guild
of Observators."
His smile widened.
"But you can call me Percy.
Now then, might you tell me who
you are and what those things are that you're carrying,
and why you are being pursued through these
hallowed corridors by armed guards?"

"I'm Esmeralda Lightfoot," said Esmeralda. "And
this is Trundle and this is Jack, and this"—she held
up the crown—"is the Crystal Crown of the Badger
Lords of Old, whether you believe me or not!"

"Why should I not believe you?" Percy asked
mildly.

"Well, your boss didn't," said Jack.

"He ordered us out of his office and set the guards on us!" added Trundle.

"Ah, well, His Nibs is not at his best if his mid-morning nap is interrupted," said Percy. "But even at the best of times, some of us are more open-minded than others. May I?" He lifted the crown from Esmeralda's hands and turned it slowly so that its crystals glittered and sparked. "What a lovely thing!" he said. "And where did you find it?"

"In Drune," said Esmeralda. "And this key was with it."

"We came here because one of the seals on the handle is the coat of arms of the ancient kings of Widdershins," said Trundle. "I don't suppose you'd know what the other one is?"

"We think it's a clue for finding the next crown," said Jack. "So it would be handy if you recognized it."

Percy handed the crown back to Esmeralda and took the key. He stepped over to the window and peered carefully at it in the light.

"Yes, that's definitely the escutcheon of the ancient kings," he said. "But I don't have the least idea what the other seal is."

"You mean we've come all this way for nothing?" groaned Esmeralda.

"Not at all," said Percy with a smile. "Just because I don't recognize the seal doesn't mean we won't be able to find out what it is."

"You can do that for us?" asked Trundle. "Really and truly?"

"I believe I can," said Percy. He handed the key back to Esmeralda. "Keep it safe," he told her. "We must go to the upper ancillary library annex—I think the book we need will be there. Come along with me."

He led them out of the office via a back door and

along narrow corridors lined with yet more bulging shelves.

"Excuse me for asking," Trundle ventured as they walked along, "but what exactly is it that you people do here? What are observators?"

"We're scientists," said Percy. "We measure and check and annotate, we calculate and cipher and compute, we evaluate and determine and prognosticate, we value and weigh and consider every tiny aspect of the Sundered Lands. It's our privilege and our bounden duty to create a scientific basis for everything that has ever happened in this world, and everything that is happening right now, and everything that will ever happen." He smiled. "It's quite a task, I can tell you!"

"I would imagine so," said Trundle. "Forgive me for asking . . . but *why* do you do all those things?"

"To accumulate knowledge, my lad," said Percy with a hint of pride in his voice. "It's a never-ending task, you know. For instance, the Directorate of Spatial Interluditudes has the task of measuring the distances between every single island in the whole of the Sundered Lands."

"Lawks!" said Jack.

"Lawks indeed, my fine fellow," agreed Percy. "The problem is that the islands are constantly moving about by tiny amounts, so no sooner is the chart complete than they have to start all over again."

"Phew!" Esmeralda blew out her cheeks. "What a total waste of time."

"The search for knowledge is never a waste of time!" said Percy. "Ah! Here we are. Almost there!"

He opened a door. They walked out into a wide corridor.

A bunch of armed guards were loitering nearby. They turned and raised their weapons as they saw the three friends emerge through the doorway.

"Got you!" leered one of them. "But you don't have to come quietly—in fact, make as much noise as you like! I love the sound of screaming prisoners!"

9

PERCY HELPS OUT

The three companions backed away from the looming guards, Trundle fumbling for his sword.

"What's going on here?" asked the Herald Pursuivant, coming through the doorway and looking the guards up and down.

"Escorting prisoners to the dungeons, sir," said the chief guard, standing up stiffly and saluting. "As per Doctor Brockwise's orders, sir."

"Nonsense," said Percy. "These fellows are my

new apprentice clerks. I think you must have made some kind of mistake, Sergeant Fawkes."

"Don't think so, begging your pardon, sir," said Fawkes. "We was told they'd have a crown and a key on 'em." He pointed to Esmeralda. "She's got them very objects in her mitts, sir."

"Indeed she has," agreed Percy. "They belong to my archives and are no concern of yours," he continued, a stern tone entering his voice. "And the longer you waste time bandying words with me, Fawkes, the farther from your clutches the real perpetrators will be!" His eye glinted. "Chop, chop, Sergeant! There are dangerous fugitives on the loose!"

"Yes, sir." The sergeant spun on his heel. "About face, men. Quick march!" The guards stomped off down the corridor. As they rounded the corner, Trundle saw the sergeant give the three of them a rather peeved look.

"Nice going, Percy," grinned Esmeralda.

The Herald Pursuivant now led them to a tall circular room lined with bookshelves. A spiral staircase on wheels wound its way up to the high, domed glass ceiling. In the middle of the room stood a round marble-topped table.

Percy wheeled the staircase around and then climbed up to a high shelf. Tucking a book under his arm, he came back down. He laid the book carefully on the tabletop. It was big and thick, bound with brown leather with curious patterns and designs embossed on it.

Trundle gazed at the title, picked out in gold leaf.

Ye Complyte and Uttre Tome of Insignias and Arms, Cheerfullie Illustrated

Trundle's snout wrinkled as Percy opened the book. Its dusty and musty smell tickled his nose till he wanted to sneeze.

"This book lists every coat of arms, motto, escutcheon, crest, charge, badge, and tincture ever used in heraldry," Percy explained as he turned the thick, creaking pages. "Show me the key again, Esmeralda."

She held it up so he could see the mysterious seal.

"Hmm, hmmm," he said, turning more pages. "A saltire with bars and bells, hmm, hmm."

Trundle peered around his elbow, dazzled by the number of different coats of arms on display. There were several on each page, all in full color and each with an explanation beneath in rich Gothic text.

"I think we're narrowing it down," said Percy. "It's definitely the coat of arms of one of the ancient guilds."

"How many different guilds are there?" asked Esmeralda.

"Originally, there were three thousand nine hundred and seventy-two," said Percy.

"Lummy!" exclaimed Jack. "We could be here for days!"

"I don't think so," said Percy. "The silver saltires suggest it is a guild of scientists and mechanics." He tapped at the key with a fingernail. "And those bells are the most significant of all!" He turned several more pages. "Hah! Yes, the bell is the sign of the Ancient Guild of Horologists!"

"Who-what-ogists?" asked Esmeralda.

"Clockmakers, to you," said Percy.

"It's a winding key for a clock!" said Trundle excitedly. "We never once thought of that. How marvelous!"

"Now all we need do is find the clock it was made for," added Jack.

"It must be here in Widdershins," said Esmeralda.

"I can't think that it would be anywhere else," Percy agreed. "Such a large old key must fit a large old clock."

"Are there any large old clocks around here?" asked Jack.

"Several," said Percy. "But none of them is big enough to need such an impressive key." He rubbed his chin. "This is most perplexing."

"Please, Percy—do think!" urged Esmeralda. "It must be a very big and a very special clock."

"I know, I know," mused the Herald Pursuivant. "Now, where can it be? *Wait!*" His sudden yell made Trundle jump. "The old clock tower! It's in Bodger's Quad, out by the Tower of the Swollen Gargoyles in the West Ward. Hmm, tricky."

"Why tricky?" asked Trundle.

"Because that area is out of bounds," said Percy. "No one is allowed to go there."

"Hah!" declared Esmeralda. "So someone knows something about it and wants to keep people out, eh?"

"Not exactly," said Percy. "It's out of bounds because it's falling to pieces. It's a ruin. I'm not sure we can risk going there without help. I'll go and speak with Doctor Brockwise. I'll tell him everything and suggest he equip an expeditionary party to enter Bodger's Quad. Then we can investigate slowly and safely."

"Um, Percy," said Esmeralda, "I don't think that's such a good idea. You see, we haven't told you the whole tale."

"Indeed?" said Percy, his eyebrows lifting. "Then perhaps you should."

And so Esmeralda, with interjections from Jack and Trundle, explained about Millie Rose Thorne and the pirates and how the *Iron Pig* could turn up at any minute now, which would mean unpleasantness and slaughter and similar bad things.

"So you see, Percy, we're on a bit of a deadline," finished Esmeralda.

"And on top of that," added Trundle, "we're pretty sure that Esmeralda's aunt sent a raven messenger here. It passed us on the way, and it gave me a very nasty look."

"Which means someone here may already know about us," said Esmeralda. "So the quicker we find the next crown and get out of here, the better."

"I see," said Percy. "Well, under the circumstances, I think we should definitely risk the perils of Bodger's Quad, come what may!"

Percy took them by unused routes and deserted thoroughfares right across the great expanse of the guild's property. Trundle became aware after a while that things were beginning to look rather tumble-down.

They walked along a dusty, rubbish-filled corridor. A door swung open on one hinge, leading only to a gaping hole in the ground. They crossed a courtyard surrounded by ruined buildings that reared up around them like broken teeth. Tough grasses sprouted from between pavingstones. Spiky bushes shouldered up between rotting bricks. Ivy crawled over buildings with broken glass in their eyes and with caved-in roofs like rib bones against the sky.

"This is Bodger's Quad," said Percy as the four of them squeezed through a small gap in a broken-backed arched gateway.

A square courtyard stood before them, the pavingstones rank with weeds and rustling grasses, the dilapidated buildings crawling with bell weed and thick-stemmed ivy. It smelled strongly of decay and rot. In the middle of all the dereliction, a tall square tower

rose in a cloak of ivy. At the top of the tower, just visible through ivy leaves and tendrils, was a large clockface.

"I hope the stairs are intact," said Esmeralda as they approached the tower.

She was in for a disappointment. The only entrance was clogged with rubble.

"It looks like all the innards must have collapsed years ago," said Jack disconsolately, kicking a big chunk of stone. "What a mess!"

Esmeralda stepped back and stared up through the clinging ivy.

"I suppose a brave and noble sort of person could climb up the outside," she said thoughtfully. She looked at Trundle. "What do you think?"

He opened his mouth to say that if she thought he was lunatic enough to try climbing all the way up to the top of the tower, she could think again. But he stopped. What was the point?

"I'm afraid I'm rather too old for that kind of thing," said Percy.

"I could do it," said Jack.

"No," said Trundle heavily. "I should climb up there if anyone does."

"He's quite right," said Esmeralda, looking admiringly at Trundle. "The Badger Blocks only showed the Princess in Darkness and the Lamplighter. Sorry, Jack, it's great to have you along, but the quest belongs to me and Trundle—and I'm rotten with heights." She looked at Trundle. "I'd do it otherwise," she said.

"Yes, I know you would," he replied. "All right. Stand back, everyone, here goes nothing."

"If you fall, try to go limp," said Jack. "You'll break fewer bones that way."

"Thanks," said Trundle. "I'll bear that in mind."

He took off his brown robes and handed his sword to Esmeralda. The last thing he needed was for the long blade to get tangled up in the ivy! Esmeralda gave him the key. Tucking it securely in his belt, he tested the strength of the ivy stems. They seemed to be firmly stapled to the stonework of the tower. He sighed and thought of his cozy sitting room back in Shiverstones. Adventures, he thought to himself, would be so much more pleasant if they didn't involve quite so many near-death experiences.

He began to climb, spluttering and coughing as the acrid ivy dust got into his nose. Fortunately the stems were very thick and solid, clinging on to the face of the tower with fierce rootlets that dug right in between the stones.

The unpleasant smell of rank, decaying ivy and rotting stone got right into Trundle's snout. Every now and then he had to pause to sneeze and to wipe the dust out of his eyes. He looked down, seeing the anxious faces of Percy and his two friends staring up at him from surprisingly far below.

He took a deep breath and continued to climb. His foot caught in between two stems, and he had a perilous time getting himself free again. Things got even more hazardous when he had to drag himself over a lip of stone about halfway up the tower. He hung on for dear life, muttering prayers to the Protector of all Small Mammals as he dragged himself up and over the projection while twigs and leaves and bits and pieces of stonework went raining down.

"Careful!" shouted Esmeralda, rather unnecessarily.

Trundle stared upward through the ivy leaves. Not far to go now! He tested a stem and put his weight on it. It cracked, and he was left dangling, clinging on by his fingers with his feet hanging in the air.

Terrified, he fought to keep his grip while he searched blindly with his feet for some secure hold. At last his scrabbling toes found a solid branch, and he was able to take some of the wrenching weight off his poor arms. He hung there for a few moments, gathering his wits, his heart hammering under his ribs. Then he started climbing again, shoving up through the ivy, hot and worn out and sick to death of this stupid tower.

At last he came to a wide ledge near the top of the tower. He strained up and saw that the huge clockface was directly above him. "Come on, Trundle, my lad," he panted. "You can do this!"

He struggled and kicked and shoved and heaved and hauled and squirmed and finally found himself on the ledge, his prickles all covered in twigs and leaves, his arms and legs aching, his fingers almost numb with the effort.

He heard hearty cheers from below. Clinging grimly to the ivy, he moved to the brink of the ledge and waved down. "I'm fine!" he called.

There were more cheers from below.

He was aware of thick layers of bird poo under

his feet, sticky and squishy in the heat of the day and very smelly. Yuck! he thought. That's all I needed.

He could see quite a distance from this vantage point—across the ruination of the West Ward to where towers and turrets and steeples rose into the sky and windows shone like silver in the sun.

A rusty iron rail emerged from the darkness of the ivy on one side of the tower. It ran the length of the ledge and then curved back into the hidden stonework. How odd. He wondered what it was there for. Leaning back a little, he looked up at the huge clockface behind its veil of knotted ivy. He felt dwarfed by the round white disk—even the numerals that ringed its circumference were taller than he was.

Now what? he thought to himself.

Aha! Just above the numeral VI, he saw a dark keyhole set into the clockface.

That's it! That's where the key goes!

He assumed that there must be some small

hatchway close by, through which, in ancient times, the Winder of the Clock would emerge to do his duty and to keep the clock ticking. But the clock was quite silent now, the hands tangled in ivy tendrils, the ironwork cloaked in a layer of thick red rust.

Gripping the key between his teeth, Trundle climbed up the VI. The numerals had plenty of scrollwork on them, and it wasn't too difficult to get to the top. Hanging on with one paw, Trundle took the key from between his teeth and tried to insert it in the hole.

At first it wouldn't go in. But he shoved and wriggled and pushed and poked, and finally the key slotted into place. He paused, gasping for breath, his muscles aching from the effort.

"Try turning the key!" he heard Esmeralda shout up.

"Great idea, Esmeralda," he called down with heavy sarcasm. "Why didn't I think of that?"

"Sorry. Just trying to be helpful."

Catching his breath, Trundle gripped the key and twisted. It refused to turn. He gritted his teeth and tried again, using all of his strength. Very gradually, and with a terrible grating noise, the key turned. A moment later, he heard machinery grinding into motion within the tower.

Grrrrrnnngggg. Krrrrkkkk. Screeeeeeeeech. Claaaaaaaannnkkk.

The noise was deafening, and as the workings of the huge clock slowly clanked into action, the whole tower began to shake and shudder. Trundle slipped off the top of the VI and slid down onto the ledge with a bump, clutching frantically at the ivy and almost tumbling off as the crumbling stonework shivered and quivered all around him. Chunks of masonry went crashing downward. Esmeralda and Jack and Percy had to leap away from the foot of the tower to avoid being brained by the falling debris.

And then from deep inside the tower came the clanging and clonging and dinging and donging of bells and gongs, rattling Trundle's brains until he thought his head would surely explode!

And as if that wasn't terrifying enough, he suddenly found himself in the middle of a great swarming mass of flapping black wings as entire flocks of ravens came pouring out of every hole in the top of the tower, croaking and screaming and battering him as they fled the noise.

He ducked and dodged the birds as they hurtled past him, but above the horrible din of the chiming clock, he could have sworn he heard a spiteful croak close to his ear.

"You'll be sorry!" it rasped. "You'll get yours, matey! Just you see!"

And then, while Trundle was still recovering from all the shocks that had hit him so far, the clock began to strike.

Gloiiiing!

Gloiiiing!

GLOOOOIIIINNNGG!

And at that moment, he saw the ivy being pushed outward as hidden doors opened on either side of the clockface and a procession of huge, rusty old iron statues began to emerge. Trundle gave a yelp as the figures approached him. That explained the iron rail! It was for these huge statues to run along.

The statues were of badgers dressed in full armor. As they rumbled toward him, their bodies began to move mechanically, twisting and turning, swinging swords and axes, beating at one another as though in some slow-motion battle.

Their joints screeched and crunched as they came closer to where Trundle was standing. He had no time to climb out of the way. Taking a deep breath, he flung himself at the first of the badger knights and threw both arms around the great rusty leg.

But even as he hung there, something caught
his eye.

The leading figure
had a crown around
its helmet.

An iron crown.

It wasn't a knight
at all—it was a king!

"Oh, good
heavens!" he gasped.
"I've found the Iron
Crown!"

A new sense of
excitement took over,
and he clambered
up the badger king's

body until he was perched on the high shoulders. He
reached for the crown, noticing that it was the only
part of the massive figure that was not coated in rust.

He wrestled it free of the king's head.

"Look!" he shouted down, waving the crown. "I have it! I have it!"

But then the badger king rotated on his axis, his upper body clanking forward as if bowing, and suddenly Trundle found himself hanging upside down, his feet clinging around the king's neck and the crown dangling from his fingers.

10

THE RED FEATHER

A horrible vision flashed in front of Trundle's eyes as he swung upside down from the badger king's neck. He saw himself being carried into the dark and noisy workings of the clock. He saw himself caught up in the cogwheels and levers and hammers. He saw himself being mashed to a pulp and spat out as hedgehog meatballs!

But a moment later, the whole promenade of iron knights came to a juddering, screeching halt. The mechanism had jammed. The badger king jerked and shuddered, almost shaking Trundle loose.

Esmeralda's frantic voice came up to him. "Throw down the crown!" she hollered. "Free your hands!"

He twisted his head and saw the three of them down there, waving and yelling. "A-a-all ri-i-ight. Ma-a-ake sure you ca-a-a-atch it!" he called down, his voice shaken to pieces by the jarring vibrations of the iron king.

"I will!" hollered Esmeralda.

Trundle let go of the crown. Esmeralda stood beneath it, her arms stretched up. But at the last second she dived to one side. The crown struck the paving stones with a mighty *cloiiiing* and went bouncing across the courtyard.

Trundle was appalled! He was convinced that he saw something break off the crown as it bowled through the tall grass and weeds with Jack in close pursuit. What was Esmeralda thinking? Why hadn't she caught it?

He was so annoyed with her that he swung down from the iron king's neck, clambered down his body, and made a swift descent of the ivy-clad tower without once thinking of how dangerous it was.

"You loon!" he shouted at Esmeralda. "Why did you jump out of the way?"

"The sun got in my eyes!" retorted Esmeralda. "I couldn't see properly! You should have waited till I was ready!"

Trundle stared at her. "I should have hung there by my toes till you were *ready*?" he exclaimed. "Are you out of your mind?"

"Not too much harm done," called Jack, running toward them with the slightly dented crown in one hand and something circular in the other.

Trundle looked at the round object. It was the orb, broken off the top of the crown.

"May I see it?" asked Percy. Jack handed him the crown and the orb. Percy held the metal ball up to the light and turned it slowly in his fingers.

"Interesting," he said. "Very interesting." He showed it to the three friends. "Do you see? It has a line running around it. I think it's made from two separate pieces." He shook it gently. "I think I can hear something moving inside."

"Open it!" cried Esmeralda.

"I'll try," said Percy. "But it might be wise to move away from the tower—if only for the sake of our ears!"

He had a point. Even down here, the noise was earsplitting, and the grating of the trapped mechanism was so violent that Trundle half feared it would shake the entire tower to pieces.

They moved away. Percy handed Esmeralda the crown and took the iron orb in both hands. He gave a sharp twist. There was a squeak of metal rubbing on metal, and the two halves of the orb fell apart.

"Ooooh!" breathed Esmeralda, staring into the two hollow shells of the orb. "What's that?"

One of the hemispheres had something wound up inside it. Something red.

Very carefully Esmeralda picked the thing out. It immediately uncoiled and revealed itself to be a very long, bright red feather.

"Oh!" she gasped, bringing her other hand up to hold the stem of the feather. "It's trying to get away!"

Trundle could see what she meant. The tip of the long feather was straining away from her, as though it wanted to pull itself free.

"Why is it doing that?" Trundle asked.

Jack was hopping excitedly from foot to foot. "I know what it is!" he cried. "Oh my gosh and golly! I never thought I'd ever see the like! It's as beautiful as it says in the songs!"

"What songs?" asked Esmeralda, struggling with the maverick feather. "What is it?"

"It's a phoenix feather!" exclaimed Jack. "Haven't you ever heard the songs?" And so saying, he began to sing.

> *O glorious and majestic bird*
> *In a golden nest at the end of the world!*
> *Most beautiful and wise and kind—*
> *Blessed is he who can the phoenix find.*

> *A feather red he left at rest*
> *When away he flew to build his nest.*
> *If secrets you seek, take the feather to the bird.*
> *Ask the phoenix wise and hear his word.*

> *You must sail away for a year and a day*
> *Into lonely lands where no beast does stray—*
> *Before he bursts into splendid fire,*
> *The lovely phoenix will grant your desire.*

"It's a very old song indeed," Jack explained. "Hundreds of years old! But I never thought it was a true story."

"Does that mean the phoenix bird knows a secret he'll tell you if you give him his feather back?" asked Esmeralda.

"That's what the old song says," agreed Jack.

"What do you think, sir?" Trundle asked the Herald Pursuivant.

"I think the old song may well tell the truth," said Percy. "I have certainly read ancient scripts concerning the mystical and magnificent phoenix bird. If I remember correctly, the phoenix is said to live inside a fiery mountain on a bleak and lonely island far from the sun." He shook his head. "But as for how you are to get there—I'm afraid I have no idea at all."

"We don't need to know," said Esmeralda. "The feather knows. Look!" She walked up and down, turning this way and that. "Do you see?" she said. "Whichever way I turn, the feather always wants to go the same way."

She was right. No matter which way she moved, the fluffy tip of the feather twisted and strained as though desperate to fly off in one particular direction.

"The feather will lead us to the phoenix nest!" said Jack. "Oh, how wonderful!"

"And I bet the phoenix knows the location of the third crown," added Esmeralda. "The Crown of Fire!"

"How very exciting!" exclaimed Percy. "I think you should go back to your skyboat and prepare to set sail immediately."

"Yes! We will," said Esmeralda.

Trundle felt a stab of guilt. He stepped up to the Herald Pursuivant. "Excuse me, sir, you've been so kind and helpful that I think we ought to make a confession."

"And what might that be, my lad?" asked Percy.

"We knocked the door guard out," explained Trundle. "He's locked up in the guardhouse, tied up with his own trousers. Sorry about that."

"We gagged him with a sock," added Esmeralda.

"He was trying to cut us all into chunks with his ax," said Jack. "So it was self-defense, really."

"I see," said Percy gravely. "That's probably quite a serious offense." He looked thoughtful for a moment. "Well, well, I can't stand those guards, and I believe you to be good and honest beasts, so let's say no more about it. But under the circumstances, I think it's even more important that you get out of here as quickly as possible. I know a quiet little side gate you can slip out of."

"Thank you," said Esmeralda. "Listen, I know you've already helped us a lot, but I was wondering if you could do one more thing for us? It's these crowns, you see. They're not exactly easy to hide, and I'm worried that someone might come along and steal them from us. So I was wondering whether you'd be prepared to look after them for us?"

"I'm most flattered that you should trust me with something so important," said Percy, "but I really can't."

"Oh, please do," said Trundle. "Otherwise we're going to have to carry them around with us wherever we go. And they're not exactly light, you know."

"And we have four more to find," added Jack.

"Please?" asked Esmeralda.

"Well, if you insist, then I shall," said Percy. "There is a chest in my office that is always kept locked. The only key is kept on a chain around my neck. I'll put the crowns there for you till you return."

"Thank you," they all chorused. "Thank you so much!"

"One last thing," said Esmeralda. "If a nice, kindly looking old Roamany lady comes by asking after us . . . don't tell her a *thing*!"

"I shall deny all knowledge of you," said the Herald Pursuivant. "And now, away you go, my fine young friends. Your quest awaits!"

He led them to a small gate and waved farewell as they made their way down the narrow, sloping streets of Widdershins.

Trundle waved back, glad to know that the two crowns would be kept safe.

The sun was just setting as they climbed on board the *Thief in the Night*. Jack unfurled the sail and Esmeralda took the tiller, and in no time at all they went darting up into the evening sky.

Trundle stood in the bows, the long red feather held between his paws. As Esmeralda turned the tiller, the feather writhed in Trundle's grip and strained off away from the setting sun.

"To the world's end!" cried Esmeralda as she turned the skyboat to follow the feather. "To the nest of the glorious phoenix bird, and to the hiding place of the Crown of Fire!"

And even as she spoke, the sails filled with the wind, and the *Thief in the Night* went skimming off to new adventures.